"Are you sleeping?" Linda asked.

"Hardly! I was trying to decide if I should let you sleep in your car, or if I should play the gentleman and offer you my bed—without me in it, of course," Mac replied.

"You'll play the gentleman," she said, her smile disturbingly sweet. "Of course."

"What makes you so sure?"

"I've got you figured out."

"Don't try to second-guess me, cookie. I'm not that easy to read." He ran his fingertips over his jaw. "I've been going over a few things in my mind."

She sat motionless, her clear blue eyes huge in her face.

"I'll help you find your missing niece," he said.

She sagged against the cushions, her relief manifest. "If you do that, there's nothing I won't do for you in return."

"Be careful what you promise."

CATHERINE SPENCER, once an English teacher, fell into writing through eavesdropping on a conversation about Harlequin® romances. Within two months she had changed careers, and sold her first book to Harlequin in 1984. She moved to Canada from England thirty years ago and lives in Vancouver. She is married to a Canadian and has two daughters and two sons—plus a dog and a cat. In her spare time she plays the piano, collects antiques and grows tropical shrubs.

Books by Catherine Spencer

HARLEQUIN PRESENTS®
2101—THE UNEXPECTED WEDDING GIFT
2143—ZACHARY'S VIRGIN
2172—PASSION'S BABY
2197—MISTRESS ON HIS TERMS
2269—THE PREGNANT BRIDE

Don't miss any of our special offers. Write to us at the following address for information on our newest releases.

Harlequin Reader Service
U.S.: 3010 Walden Ave., P.O. Box 1325, Buffalo, NY 14269
Canadian: P.O. Box 609, Fort Erie, Ont. L2A 5X3

Catherine Spencer

MACKENZIE'S PROMISE

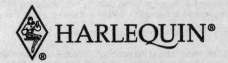

TORONTO • NEW YORK • LONDON
AMSTERDAM • PARIS • SYDNEY • HAMBURG
STOCKHOLM • ATHENS • TOKYO • MILAN • MADRID
PRAGUE • WARSAW • BUDAPEST • AUCKLAND

ISBN 0-373-12286-1

MACKENZIE'S PROMISE

First North American Publication 2002.

Copyright © 2002 by Kathy Garner.

This edition published by arrangement with Harlequin Books S.A.

® and TM are trademarks of the publisher. Trademarks indicated with
® are registered in the United States Patent and Trademark Office, the
Canadian Trade Marks Office and in other countries.

Visit us at www.eHarlequin.com

Printed in U.S.A.

CHAPTER ONE

THE day they shipped her sister off by ambulance to the psychiatric wing of Lion's Gate Hospital was the day Linda Carr decided to take matters into her own hands. The police had had their chance and, as far as she could tell, were getting precisely nowhere. Bad enough that the baby had been missing for seven weeks now; to stand idly by while June retired farther into the fuzzy world of tranquilizers was not to be countenanced.

Not that Linda blamed her sister. She'd known her own share of sleepless nights since the infant girl had disappeared, and she could only imagine how much worse it had been for the new mother to be told that her firstborn had been smuggled out of the hospital nursery—by the father, no less!

It shouldn't have come as a surprise that Kirk Thayer would resort to extreme measures. From all accounts, he'd shown an astonishing lack of moderation in most things to do with June, practically from the day he'd learned she was expecting his child. It was the main reason she'd refused to marry him. But that he'd go so far as to kidnap the baby and disappear without trace...!

"I'll bring your little daughter home," Linda promised, when she visited June the morning after she'd been hospitalized. "You just concentrate on getting well so that you're ready to be a mommy, and leave the rest to me."

"And how do you propose to do that?" Linda's friend Melissa asked that night, as the two of them dined on pasta primavera at their favorite West Vancouver restaurant. "Being a bona fide European-trained chef doesn't exactly qualify you as a private investigator. It's already been established that Thayer left town the same day he stole the baby and probably returned to the States. He could be anywhere by now, and given his unpredictable state of mind, I think you're going to need an expert to track him down.''

"Uh-uh!" Linda shook her head decisively. "Not *an* expert, *the* expert—and I've got you to thank for finding him for me. Remember that magazine article you sent to me when I was living in Rome—the one you wrote about the maverick police officer who quit the force because he refused to be bound by all the red tape surrounding it?''

Melissa eyed her incredulously. "Please tell me you're not referring to the reclusive Mac Sullivan, former ace detective now living in exclusive solitude on the Oregon coast.''

"The very same. Going through the conventional channels isn't working. It's time for a more radical approach.''

"Quite possibly it is, but Mac Sullivan's not your man. He won't even return your phone calls, much less agree to help you. I'd even go so far as to say that he's the most bullheaded creature on earth, and I know whereof I speak. Researching that article was worse than pulling hen's teeth. Setting up a private tell-all interview with the Queen of England would have been easier.''

"I don't care. He's the acknowledged expert when it comes to tracking down missing persons—practically clairvoyant, according to your article—and I'm prepared to camp on his doorstep so that he trips over me every time he sets foot outside his house, if necessary. It beats sitting on my hands and watching June turn into a wraith of the woman she used to be.''

"I can't say I blame you. I barely recognized her the last time I saw her. She's nothing but skin and bone. And those haunted eyes…!'' Melissa inspected her glass of wine and let out an exaggerated sigh. "So what can I do to help— since I assume that's why you're bribing me with this very fine merlot?''

"I want you to check your sources and find out exactly

where this Sullivan man lives. I need something a bit more specific than 'on the Oregon coast', which covers a lot of territory.''

"I don't need to check any sources for that. He lives right on the beach in Trillium Cove.''

"Never heard of it.''

"Not many people have. It lies between Bandon and Coos Bay, and caters to the rich and reclusive, not tourists or newshounds. We were treated like lepers when we started nosing around town. Your best bet, if you're determined to go this route, is to be discreet and look sophisticated, which shouldn't be too difficult, given your worldly, cosmopolitan air. It's a small town and none of the streets have names, so there's no point in looking at a map. On the plus-side, though, his place lies at the end of a gravel road running directly west of the post office, so you'll find it easily enough. But for what it's worth, if you do find him—''

"When," Linda corrected her. "I *will* find him, Melissa. I have to. June can't go on like this and neither, come to that, can our mother. She's been sick with worry for weeks now and the stress…well, you know how much she has to put up with already. This could be the last straw for her.''

"Then *when* you find him, don't rush your fences.''

"Why not? This is an emergency and time's of the essence. What's wrong with being up-front about that?''

"Trillium Cove isn't Rome or Paris—or even Vancouver. Things don't happen at breakneck speed around there just because you want them to—and Mac Sullivan's definitely not someone to be pushed. You can't go hammering on his door and expect the only thing he'll ask is 'How high?' just because you tell him to jump. If there was one thing which came across loud and clear during the brief interview he granted us, it's that his priority these days is completing the book he's writing on criminal profiles, and he resents anything which takes time away from that, although he did admit to doing a bit of police consulting on the side, once in a very rare while.''

"He'll make an exception when I explain what happened. He has to."

"Uh-uh!" Melissa scooped up a forkful of pasta and shook her head decisively. "He doesn't *have* to do anything. This is a man who values both his privacy and his freedom to pick and choose how he spends his time."

"He'll choose this case when he finds out how much I'm prepared to pay."

Again, Melissa shook her head. "He's also filthy rich. It takes more zeroes than I earn in three months to pay the taxes on that property of his, let alone afford all the other little perks he enjoys. No, kiddo. To get him to take an interest in your case, you're going to have to adopt a sneakier method and be *very* persuasive—if you get my drift!"

Linda's stared at her, affronted. "I hope you're not implying I *come* on to him?"

"I wouldn't have put it quite like that, but since you did, then yes. In a way."

"Fat chance! The day has yet to dawn when—"

"I'm suggesting you stroke his ego, not show up stark naked and offer to give him a full body massage, for heaven's sake!"

"No!" Linda was adamant. She'd fended off romantic overtures from infatuated master chefs and five-star restaurateurs with equal dispatch during her years of training abroad, and wasn't about to compromise her standards now for some small-town ex-police officer with an overblown sense of his own importance. "Apart from the principle of the thing, I can't afford the time for those kinds of games."

"You can't afford not to! And if appealing to his vanity gets the results you're after, what's another couple of days?" Melissa's tone softened. "Look, Linda, I know better than anyone that this isn't how you usually operate. You're the most straightforward person I've ever met—to a fault, sometimes. But there's nothing usual about what's happened to your family. It's cruel and heartbreaking and scary beyond any normal person's wildest imaginings, and if you want to put an end to the misery, the only thing you can afford to focus on is bringing your niece home safely and seeing that Kirk Thayer is brought to justice.''

Linda chewed on that for a while, then sighed deeply. ''Loath though I am to admit it, I'm afraid you might be right,'' she said, not much liking it but realistic enough to recognize there was no getting away from the truth of Melissa's analysis. ''If flattery will bring Mac Sullivan on board, I'll butter him up one side and down the other so thoroughly, he'll glow. I'll do whatever it takes, and worry about my methods when that baby is back in her mother's arms where she belongs.''

''And I wish you luck. Because, believe me, you'll need lots of it.''

Even in mid-August, after weeks of hot, dry weather, the ocean was cold. Enough that Mac wore a wet suit when he rode the Windsurfer, though not enough to keep him from his early-morning swim. He needed that bracing dash into the icy waves to clear the cobwebs from his brain and prepare him for the day's work. One thousand words minimum before four in the afternoon, fifteen hundred if he was lucky—and that didn't count the research, or the pages of notes he compiled before he tackled the latest chapter.

The surf was wilder than usual that day, requiring he keep his attention on what he was doing, which probably explained why he wasn't aware someone had invaded his section of beach until he practically stepped on her as he waded ashore.

Still half-blinded by the glare of sun on water, Mac detected the visitor was a woman only by her voice. Clear, bossy, cultured, it accosted him as he hoisted the Windsurfer under one arm and prepared to climb the steps to the house. ''Watch what you're doing with that thing! You just about took my head off!''

''A danger you could have avoided if you'd paid attention to your whereabouts,'' he informed her murky silhouette. ''You're on private property, lady.''

''How am I supposed to know that?''

He jerked his head to indicate the signs nailed to the twisted trunks of the scrub pines edging the low-rising dune. ''You could try reading—assuming you know how.''

His vision clearer by then, he watched with grim amusement as she reared back in outrage. ''I'd heard you were a bit short on social graces,'' she huffed, ''but I'd no idea you were such a Neanderthal.''

''Well, now that you've been enlightened, why don't you go back to wherever you came from and leave me to grunt in peace?''

''Because,'' she said, and faltered into silence.

She had wide-spaced blue-green eyes almost the color of the sea close-in to shore. Blond hair framing a heart-shaped face in a halo of short curls. Full, stubborn mouth, dimpled chin. Slight build, shapely legs, about five-four in her bare feet, and weighing around a hundred and ten pounds. Fingers braided so tightly together it was a wonder they didn't dislocate. Twenty-sixish, possibly a bit younger. A very uptight woman.

He noticed all that not because he gave a damn but because he'd been trained to observe. Eleven years on the police force stayed with a man, even after he turned in his badge.

'' 'Because' isn't a reason,'' he said.

She looked down at her knotted fingers. ''I'm sorry if I'm trespassing. I really didn't notice the signs.''

''I don't see how you could miss them. They're in plain enough sight.''

She took that under consideration for a minute, then drummed up an obsequious smile and said, ''But so were you. And I was captivated watching you on the Windsurfer. You're amazing.''

''So I've been told—by women a lot more subtle than you.''

She blushed, the color running up under her honey-gold skin and leaving her looking like a kid caught dipping into the cookie jar behind her mother's back. "I'm not trying to flirt with you."

"Sure you are," he said. "You're just not doing it very well. So why don't you spit out whatever it is you're really after, and get it over with?"

"I need your help. My sister's baby has been stolen by the father, and she's beside herself."

Mac repressed a sigh and turned to stare out at the rolling ocean, preferring its eternal tumult to the unending stream of human misery which hounded him no matter how much he tried to distance himself from it. "He's probably just taken off for the day. He'll come home again as soon as he realizes it's time for a diaper change."

"No," she said. "You don't understand. He's not my sister's husband. They don't live together. He stole the baby right out of the hospital nearly two months ago when she was only one day old, and no one's heard from him since."

Oh, jeez! "Then you should have called in the police long before now."

"We did." The bossy tone had disintegrated into something too close to despair for his peace of mind. "But it's been seven weeks, Mr. Sullivan, and they haven't made much progress."

"What makes you think I can do any better?"

"Your reputation speaks for itself."

Again he turned away, unable to confront the unwarranted hope in that wide-eyed gaze. Not many things touched him anymore, but a child gone missing, a newborn ripped from its mother's arms, and by the estranged father no less, touched a sore spot which no amount of time seemed able to heal. Any guy who would pull a stunt like that should be strung up!

"You haven't done your homework," he told her, not a hint of emotion in his voice. "If you had, you'd know I retired from active duty three years ago. But there are any number of private investigators who'll take your case and I'll be happy to refer you."

"I don't want them, I want you."

"You're wasting your time. I can't help you."

"Can't—or won't?"

Mac spun around, the ghost of a lost child's cry echoing through his mind. "Look, Ms....."

"Carr," she supplied. "Linda Carr. And my niece's name is Angela. She weighed six pounds, eleven ounces at birth and was nineteen inches long. But all that will have changed in seven weeks. She probably looks nothing like the photo taken only hours after she was born. Her mother doesn't know if she's thriving, if she's well cared for, if she's gaining weight the way she's supposed to. She doesn't even know that she's still alive."

"If the father's the kidnapper, the baby's probably fine. What reason has he to harm her?"

"What reason had he to steal her?"

"Presumably because there was trouble between him and the mother."

She nodded. "Yes. Their relationship fell apart a couple of months before Angela was born."

"Is she your sister's first child?"

"Yes, but Kirk's second. He has a son from a previous marriage whom he rarely sees because the boy lives with the ex-wife who returned to Australia after the divorce."

"That probably explains it, then. The guy probably feared he'd be denied access to this child, too."

"I really don't care what he feared, Mr. Sullivan," she said, the bossiness returning full force to her tone and setting his teeth on edge. "I care about my sister who's on the verge of complete mental collapse. And I care about a baby being left to the uncertain mercies of a man who's clearly unbalanced. I should think, if you have a grain of compassion in your soul, that you'd care, too."

"I can't take on the world's problems and make them my own, Ms. Carr," he said wearily. "I've got enough to do fighting my own demons. The best I can do for you is recommend that you hire someone who specializes in locating missing persons, and if this man's been gone nearly two months already, then the sooner you get on it, the better.''

Mac didn't wait to hear all her reasons for ignoring his advice, nor did he tell her that with every passing day the chances of the baby being recovered grew slimmer, because he wasn't getting any more involved. Period.

To underline the fact, he cleared the dunes and marched up the steps, surfboard and all, and left her to figure out another game plan, confident he'd closed the door on any possibility that it would include him.

Well, so much for subterfuge and sweet talk! Totally deflated, Linda stared at his departing back.

Why hadn't Melissa warned her?

Why hadn't she mentioned that Mac Sullivan was no ordinary man, that he had the face of a fallen angel and the body of a god? Why hadn't she seen fit to point out that his voice flowed over a woman like molasses, dark and rich and bittersweet?

Disgusted with herself, with her inappropriate susceptibility, Linda buried her face in her hands. Melissa wasn't to blame, she herself was, for having been fool enough to pin labels on him, sight unseen.

She'd read too many novels about hard-bitten, granite-jawed, flinty-voiced detectives, that was her trouble. Seen too many movies of officers with thick middles and double chins slurping coffee and demolishing doughnuts in between reading people their rights. Spent too many hours talking to the RCMP and local police who were hamstrung by protocol.

She'd come here believing she was prepared—and found she was prepared for nothing: not the endless drive lasting nearly two days; not the interminable congestion of the I-5, which had her clutching the steering wheel in a white-knuckled grip all the way from north of Seattle to Olympia; not the snaking coastal road crowded with tourists in Oregon. And definitely not Mac Sullivan.

Even her final destination was alien. She'd grown up in Vancouver, Canada's third largest city. She'd apprenticed in New York and New Orleans, in Paris and Rome. And felt more at home in any one of those cities than she did on this empty stretch of beach bordered on one side by the wild ocean and the other by sand dunes rising twenty feet or more in places.

For all her world travel and supposed sophistication, she was truly a stranger in a strange land. And no closer to finding June's baby now than she had been on her native turf.

Exhaustion swept over her, softening the edges of her disgust with the threat of tears. She'd been so sure, so determined she'd succeed where the police had failed. All during the drive south, she'd rehearsed how she'd approach Mac Sullivan, what she'd say. And been blindsided before she'd even opened her mouth. Spellbound by his commanding presence, commanding looks, commanding everything!

An image of June staring sightlessly out of her hospital room window, and another of a newborn's sweetly sleeping face, were shamefully eclipsed by the more recent memory of a man emerging from the rolling surf and striding up the beach. Of him shaking the saltwater from his dark hair and sending the drops flying around his head in a shimmering halo. Of a pair of magnificent shoulders and long, powerful legs. Of eyes glowing smoky blue-gray in his darkly tanned face.

Oh, fatigue was making a fool of her! What other explanation could there be for the way her mind had emptied of everything that mattered and fastened instead on the physical attributes of a stranger? Why else was she slumped on a chunk of driftwood, with no place to stay that night and no clue as to what her next move should be?

Already the sun was sliding down on the horizon, allowing a hint of pre-autumn chill to permeate the air. She was hungry and travel-worn and disconcerted. She needed a comfortable hotel room, a hot bath, a good dinner, and an even better night's sleep to fortify her for the battle ahead. But she knew from her earlier exploration that she'd find none of those things in Trillium Cove. The only inn in town had displayed a discreet No Vacancy sign and from what she'd seen, there weren't any restaurants.

"Stop wallowing in self-pity!" she ordered herself. "It's as unattractive as it's unproductive. Get up off your behind and do *something* because you're accomplishing nothing with this attitude!"

But her normal resilience had hit an all-time low. The accrued worry and frustration of the last few weeks had finally caught up with her and no amount of self-reproach could chase it away. Discouraged, dejected, she rested her chin on her folded arms and stared blankly at the empty horizon.

Damn her anyway! How long was she going to sit there like a lost mermaid waiting for the tide to sweep her back out to sea?

Irritated as much with himself as with her, Mac leaned back in the wicker recliner, propped his feet on the deck railing and took a healthy swig of his bourbon. Usually, topping off the day with an ounce of Jack Daniel's and a perfect sunset was all he needed to give him a sense of well-being beyond anything money could buy.

Usually.

Usually, though, he didn't have a desperate woman spoiling the view. He didn't have a woman at all, except by choice, and even then only occasionally. And he made sure whoever she was didn't come loaded down with expectations he had no intention of meeting.

Raising his glass, he squinted at the prisms of late-afternoon sunlight spearing the amber liquid. Fine stuff,

Jack Daniel's! Drink enough of it, and a guy could sink into a hazy stupor which nothing could penetrate. Trouble was, he'd learned long ago that when the effects of too much booze wore off, all he had left was a thundering headache and the same old problem he'd tried to elude to begin with. Which brought him back full circle to the woman on the—on *his*—beach.

Thoroughly ticked off, he slapped the glass down on the table at his side, lunged to his feet, and glared at her. She hadn't moved a muscle in the last half hour. Head bent, shoulders bowed, she sat sunk in palpable misery. But what irked him beyond measure was that despite there being no law which said he had to make her problems his, the sight of her remained superimposed on the forefront of his mind regardless, and his thoughts kept turning to the problem she was trying to resolve.

If it had been an errant husband she was chasing after, or someone who'd taken her for a whack of money, he'd have been able to dismiss her without a second thought. But a child…a helpless baby gone missing? A man had to have traveled a long way down the road of indifference to turn his back on that.

He had the wherewithal to help her: contacts in high places, should he need them; knowledge and experience by the bushel right at his fingertips. But he'd laid down a set of rules by which he'd sworn to live. Rules which spared him having to call on any such resources.

It was fear, not rules, which held him back now, though. Fear that all he could do at this stage was discover she'd left it too late. Fear that, at the end of it all, the only thing she'd be taking back to her sister was a miniature white casket holding a baby's remains.

He couldn't go through that a second time.

Restlessly he paced the length of the deck and back, then turned for one last glance down at the beach. It lay deserted, not just directly below the house, but as far as the eye could see to either side. Not a living soul marred the two-mile expanse of sand he called his backyard.

She'd given up. Gone back to wherever she'd come from, or else in search of someone else's help. He could eat dinner with a clear conscience. Praise the Lord!

His kitchen faced southeast, with a patio beyond the sliding glass door which caught the morning sun. He kept his barbecue out there, a gas-powered luxury model designed for year-round use regardless of the weather, but especially suited for an evening such as this.

He'd pulled a steak from the freezer and was in the process of searching the refrigerator for salad fixings when the bronze knocker on his front door struck the solid plank of oak. Not loudly or confidently or imperatively, the way he'd have approached it, but with a timid little *pflunk!*

The sixth sense which had served him so long and so well during his years on the force clicked into gear. Muttering a few choice words not fit to be heard in decent company, he strode through the living area to the hall, already resigned to what he knew he'd find waiting outside.

"Please," was all she said when he opened the door, and he was lost. Lost in the bruised shade of her eyes, more blue than green in the descending twilight. And lost in that simple entreaty which spoke more poignantly than a flood of more urgent and articulate pleas.

"I should have realized you couldn't disappear into thin air quite that fast," he said, gesturing her inside.

She was shivering, pale, and just about ready to drop in her tracks. He grasped her upper arm and was shocked at how chilled her skin felt—far more than the cooling outside temperature merited. Shocked, too, by her air of frailty. "When did you last eat?" he inquired sharply.

She thought about it for a second, then said, "I stopped for coffee this morning."

"I'm talking about a square meal."

"I don't know." She lifted her shoulders indifferently. "Last night, I guess."

Mac swore again, and propelled her to the leather couch in front of the fireplace. "Sit!" he ordered, and after she responded to the command like a well-trained member of the dog squad, he grabbed the knitted afghan his mother had sent him and flung it around her shoulders.

She curved herself into its warmth and blinked. She had the longest damned eyelashes he'd ever seen. Indulging in a few more choice obscenities—old police habits died hard—he knelt to put a match to the wood and kindling already laid in the fire grate then, while the flames took hold, returned to the kitchen and heated water to make a mug of his special hot rum toddy.

"Here," he said, marching back to the living room some five minutes later. But she was already zonked out. Head cushioned against the arm of the couch, feet tucked under her, she slept like a baby.

Parking the rum toddy on the edge of the hearth, he piled a couple more logs on the fire, then leaned against the mantel shelf and rolled his eyes in disgust. He'd grown accustomed to his comfort zone, in which he was responsible only for himself; accountable only to himself. Still, he retained just enough humanity to be touched by her troubles.

A child had gone missing, for God's sake, and even he—*especially* he!—knew the burden that cast on a person's shoulders. And he was afraid. Afraid of his response to a woman so full of need that someone had to step in on her behalf, because she couldn't do it alone. Afraid because, of all the people she could have turned to, she'd chosen him.

He'd looked into her eyes and remembered them not for their clarity of color or symmetry of shape, but for the faith he'd seen in them, and for the grief. And he was afraid of failing again.

"Jeez!" he growled. "Why me? Of all the people living along this stretch of coastline, why the hell did I have to open my door to this particular stray?"

She stirred. Puffed a little breath between her lips.

Sighed. And settled more comfortably into the corner of the couch.

Sighing himself, he stalked back to the kitchen and yanked open the freezer in search of another steak. No point in deluding himself. She was there for the duration, whether or not he liked it.

But lest there be any doubt, he liked it not one bit and intended driving the message home to her as soon as she was alert enough to comprehend it—which, given her present comatose state, was unlikely to be anytime soon.

CHAPTER TWO

THE eerie sense that she was being watched—scrutinized with unblinking intent, in fact—penetrated the mists of sleep and lent an even greater edge of danger to the fitful dreams chasing her.

Jarring awake, she sat up too suddenly and took a moment to get her bearings. Leather warm and smooth as satin against her bare skin, a soft wool shawl caressing her shoulders, a tingling numbness creeping down her right leg. Her face touched by the heat from a fire whose flames danced in reflection on the wall of windows to her left. A framed painting above the mantelpiece, of majestic evergreens marching up a mountainside. Massive beams supporting a high ceiling. Music—a Chopin nocturne, she guessed—flowing from a sound system housed in an open cabinet made of some dark wood inlaid with ivory.

And in a tanned face of incomparable male beauty, cool watchful eyes the color of storm clouds, dissecting her, feature by feature.

He lounged in a chair on the opposite side of the granite hearth, an old-fashioned glass one-third full held negligently in one hand. He'd showered and changed since he admitted her to the house. His hair gleamed thick and black against his skull, and she detected a faint and pleasant whiff of aftershave. He wore a long-sleeved shirt almost the exact shade of his eyes, and black cargo pants.

Relaxed and casual, one might have been fooled into believing. Except there was nothing relaxed or casual in his unswerving observation, and she knew without a shadow of doubt that, had the need arisen, he'd have uncoiled out of that chair in a stunning blur of speed and power. He was

20

part man, part machine; frighteningly intelligent, and terrifyingly detached.

"How long have I been asleep?" she asked him, her voice croaking from a throat grown dry and gritty.

"Close to an hour."

"You should have woken me."

"Why?"

"Because..." she said, then, unable to come up with a reason that didn't sound either affected or downright silly, drifted into silence.

"I already told you once, 'because' isn't a reason."

She wished he'd divert that unnerving stare to some place other than her face. She felt like a butterfly pinned under a microscope. Helpless. At his complete mercy. "I guess I was tired."

"I guess you were." He shifted in the chair, glanced briefly at his glass, took a mouthful of whatever he was drinking, and resumed his inspection of her. "You'd like to tidy up," he said, not in question but in command. "There's a washroom to the right of the front door."

Normally she'd have resented his tone but it had been hours since she'd been to the toilet and nature was calling with growing insistence. Wincing, she unfolded herself from the couch and slid to her feet, the pins and needles shooting up her right leg rendering it excruciatingly sensitive to the pressure.

"Cramps," she offered, feeling some sort of explanation was called for as she took a lurching step forward.

"You mean you've got your period?" he inquired dispassionately. "Sorry, I don't keep supplies like that on hand."

She thought she'd die. Scarlet in the face and probably over every other inch of exposed skin as well, she groped her way to the end of the couch. "Cramps in my leg," she stammered, beating as dignified a retreat as she could manage.

The washroom bore the same stamp of masculine opulence as the living area. Pristine white marble floor tiles, dark green porcelain fixtures, brass fittings and black hand towels. Above the sink, a large oval mirror revealed a map of creases down one side of her face and her hair mashed unflatteringly against her head from where she'd lain on it.

No wonder he'd been staring at her so fixedly. He probably hadn't seen anything quite as unsightly since the last time he'd scraped a drunk off the sidewalk, back in the days when he cruised the streets in a patrol car.

She did the best she could with soap and water, but she'd left her bag in her car at the top of his driveway and much though she'd have loved to get her hands on her toothbrush and a comb, she wasn't about to leave the house and risk not being allowed back in again. He'd just have to put up with her as she was.

"It took you long enough," he informed her, when she reappeared. "Men can do what they have to do in half the time it takes a woman."

"They also stand up to do it," she snapped without thinking, and blushed again as he let out a rumble of laughter.

"Here," he said, handing her a steaming mug. "Maybe this'll warm you up and sweeten your mood."

She sniffed the contents suspiciously. "What is it?"

"Hot rum and lemon with sugar. I just reheated it. Watch you don't burn your mouth."

"I don't like rum."

"And I don't like strays coming down with pneumonia under my roof, so do as you're told. You aren't dressed for the kind of temperatures we get out here in the evening."

"I'm not cold."

He traced the tip of his finger over her bare arm. "Then why the goose bumps?"

Because you're touching me, she thought, unable to control a shiver. "Reaction setting in after sleeping, I suppose. It's not uncommon."

"Maybe not, but I don't want to take any chances." He

tucked the knitted shawl around her shoulders and nudged her toward the fire. "Sit on the hearth awhile and down the rum while I fix us some food. You eat red meat?"

"Would it make any difference if I said 'no'?"

"Not a bit," he replied cheerfully. "I'm having steak and a baked potato, with salad and mushrooms on the side. You can either join me or watch me."

"Steak will be fine," she told him, wondering what demon of perversity made her take issue with him when what she most wanted was to win his cooperation. "Thank you for inviting me to stay."

He laughed again, unkindly this time. "As if I had any choice! Medium rare okay?"

"Perfect."

The hot rum and lemon tasted remarkably pleasant and slid down her throat in a rich, syrupy stream, warming her as thoroughly within as the fire did on the outside. Beyond an open archway at the far end of the room, she could hear him moving around, clattering utensils and running water. She found the sounds oddly comforting; a refreshing return to normality, after too many weeks fraught with anxiety and fear.

The fading glow of sunset streamed across the plain white wall opposite the windows, painting it in pastel stripes of celadon and peach. Hugging the mug in both hands, she strolled to the sliding glass doors overlooking the ocean.

The view was breathtaking, stretching as far as the eye could see over ocean and sand, cliffs and stunted, weather-bent pines. A person could gaze at the sight every day for the rest of his life, and not grow tired of the spectacle. Small wonder he'd chosen this spot as his retreat.

The huge room behind her was scarcely less impressive. *He's filthy rich,* Melissa had said, and it had been no exaggeration. In addition to the one she'd noticed above the fireplace, a number of other paintings hung on the white-washed walls, some oils, some watercolors, and every one an original. There were other items, too, which told something of his taste: a jade carving of a woman rising from a pool, her arms upstretched; a crouching mountain lion fashioned from onyx; a wide, shallow bowl of beaten copper holding a selection of bleached seashells, and a tall brass samovar.

Dark Turkish rugs left splashes of color over the pale wood floors. The leather on the couches was soft and pliant as velvet. His dining table, big enough to seat twelve with ease, gleamed with the patina of age.

"Have you lived here long?" she asked, coming to lean in the archway and watch him at work.

"Going on four years."

"It's a very handsome house. You were lucky it came on the market just when you were ready to buy."

"It didn't. I found the land and had the house built to my specifications."

"Oh." She scanned the kitchen, noting its top-of-the-line appliances, the finely crafted cabinets, the big work island with a slotted rack holding a selection of expensive knives built into one side. "Did you design the kitchen, too?"

"Right down to the last floorboard."

"I'm impressed."

"Why? Because I own more than a can opener and a frying pan?"

"No. Because most men don't have the eye for detail which you seem to possess."

"It comes with the territory," he said, separating the yolk from the white of an egg and whisking it into a bowl with olive oil, lemon juice, a little anchovy paste and a dash of Worcestershire sauce. "I used to make my living noticing details. They're critical in the solving of crime. You plan on sleeping with anybody tonight?"

She blinked, taken aback by the sudden change of subject. "I beg your pardon?"

"I asked if you planned—"

"I heard!" she said. "And I'm wondering why you think it's any of your business."

"Well not because I'm hoping you'll climb between the sheets with me, cookie, if that's what you're afraid of."

"What a relief! But that still doesn't answer my question."

With superb disregard for its razor-sharp edge, he juggled a chef's knife in his right hand, and slammed the flat side of the blade on a clove of garlic, reducing it to a pulverized mound on the chopping board. "I like plenty of this in my salad dressing. If you don't and you've got a hot and heavy night ahead, you might prefer—"

"I'll be sleeping alone."

"Oh, yeah? Where?"

"I haven't decided."

He stopped what he was doing and very deliberately fixed her once again in that daunting stare, except that this time, she detected an element of incredulity in its depths. As if he'd just discovered she was missing a vital part of her anatomy—like a brain. "Are you telling me you don't have a hotel room lined up?"

"Not yet," she admitted, trying to sound unconcerned.

"Not yet?" He raised his rather wonderful eyes heavenward as if communing with God, although he stopped short of asking, *Why me, oh Lord?* "What you really mean is you don't have the first idea where you're going to stay."

His tone and manner suggested he thought she was too mentally defective to comprehend the situation. Retaliating, she said, "I'm well aware I won't find a room right here in Trillium Cove, Mr. Sullivan."

"Congratulations," he sneered. "Are you also aware you're not likely to find one within a fifty-mile radius, because this is high tourist season and even fleabag No-Tell Motels fill up by midafternoon?"

"Should I find that to be the case, I'll sleep in my car," she said rashly.

"If that's supposed to make me feel sorry for you, you're wasting your time. There are worse things than sleeping in a car. Ask any one of the hundreds of homeless people who consider a park bench luxury accommodation." He scooped forks from a drawer, steak knives from the rack and sent the lot skimming over the work island toward her. "Here, make yourself useful, for a change. Set the table. You'll find place mats and stuff inside the sideboard in the dining area."

"Is 'please' a part of your vocabulary?" she snapped, catching the cutlery just before it flew off the granite surface and crashed to the floor. "Or didn't your mother think it necessary to teach you any manners?"

He treated her to an evil and altogether beautiful grin. "I'm a Neanderthal, remember? We don't do manners. And leave my mother out of this. She managed to raise five kids on her own without losing any of us, which is more than can be said for the family you come from."

She supposed she deserved that, but it hurt anyway. And served to remind her why she was there to begin with. If she wanted this man's help, she'd better fine-tune her approach. "I apologize," she said, swallowing her aggravation. "I shouldn't have brought your mother into this. I'm sure she's a very fine lady."

"Yes, she is," he said. "And I'm a jerk to have said what I did about your family, so that makes us even. How do you feel about California shiraz?"

She found his habit of switching subjects without warning or lead-in highly disconcerting. "To drink, you mean?"

"No, cookie. To use as shoe polish." He shook his head in mock despair. "Of course to drink—unless you don't like it any better than the rum you were so quick to denounce but which, I notice, you managed to drain to the last drop."

"I enjoy a good shiraz," she said. "Also cabernet sauvignon and pinot noir. And my name is Linda. Kindly refer to me as such—or Ms. Carr, if you prefer."

He favored her with a steely glance. "Lest we forget who's in charge around here, let's run over the ground rules. First, this is my house. Second, I didn't invite you to come here. Third, I don't take orders from anyone, particularly not a total stranger who's looking for a favor. Remember that. Cookie.''

For the space of a second or two, she glared right back, a dozen pithy retorts buzzing through her mind and begging to be aired.

Forestalling her, he grinned again. Pleasantly this time. Disarmingly so. ''Don't do it, Linda,'' he warned. ''Don't say something you'll regret. And don't gnash your teeth like that. It makes you look like a bad-tempered dog.''

''A rottweiler, I hope. One capable of ripping your throat out!''

He laughed. He was laughing, she decided, altogether too often and always at her expense. ''Afraid not. You don't have the hindquarters for it.''

She was wearing shorts, which fit trimly around her hips and showed plenty of leg, and the way he eyed her from the waist down left her in no doubt that he liked what he saw. Absurdly flattered, she blushed.

''Thought that'd soften you up,'' he said with smug satisfaction. ''Now hop to it and set the table. I'm about ready to throw these steaks on the barbecue. And one more thing: if you can do it without lopping off a finger or two, slice up that French loaf over there.''

She glared at his departing back. Much more provocation, and she'd slice him!

The steak was done to perfection, the potatoes tender and flavorful, the mushrooms, sautéed in butter and port wine, mouthwatering.

''You're a good cook,'' she said.

''I know,'' he replied with disgraceful immodesty.

''Do you eat at this table when you're alone?''

''No,'' he mocked. ''When there's no one around to watch, I get down on my hands and knees, and slurp out of a bowl on the floor.''

''You don't have to be so rude! I asked only because

your dining room furniture is so big and from everything I've learned, you aren't the kind of man who hosts large dinner parties.''

"You investigated me pretty thoroughly before you came calling, did you?''

"Enough to know you're something of a recluse and don't have many friends.''

"I have friends, Linda,'' he informed her flatly. "Not many, I admit. I prefer to be selective. As for the furniture, it was my grandmother's, and her mother's before that. The table will seat twenty when it's fully extended. They went in for lots of children in those days.''

She found it interesting that, for a man who shunned the company of others, he'd mentioned his family twice with obvious affection. "And you're one of five yourself, you said?''

"My mother had five sons.''

"And brought them up by herself? My goodness, she must have had stamina!''

"She had no choice. My father died before my youngest brother was born.''

"Oh, how tragic! What happened?''

"Nosy, aren't you?''

"I don't mean to be insensitive. But the story is so…moving. A woman alone, with five little boys, one of them a baby who never got to meet his father…'' She swallowed, the whole concept hitting a little too close to home.

"My father was a police officer killed in the line of duty.''

"Is that why you joined the force?''

"Yes,'' he said brusquely. "He was my hero. I was ten when he died, and I remember him very well. He was a good man, a good father. My mother's family were true monied blue bloods and never understood why she wanted to marry a cop when she could have had a life of ease with any number of other men. But she adored him and he her.''

"She never remarried?''

"With five boys?" he scoffed. "Even the men my grand-parents tried to line her up with after she was widowed weren't interested in taking on a gang like us, any more than she was interested in finding another husband. She'd had the best, she always said, and knew there'd never be another like him—except, possibly, for his sons who resembled him so closely that she couldn't have forgotten him, even if she'd wanted to."

Unexpectedly touched, Linda said, "It's a sad but lovely story, Mr. Sullivan. It makes me doubly regret that comment I made earlier about your mother. She sounds quite remarkable."

Actually, "superhuman" was probably closer to the mark, if her eldest son was anything to go by. He displayed a sophistication and certain male elegance strangely at odds with the tough resilience which was the legacy of his days as a police detective.

Watching him from beneath her lashes, she admired the lean, clean grace of his hands as he lifted his glass, and wondered if he handled a firearm with the same deft panache he brought to the dinner table. She suspected that he did; that even under extreme duress, he endowed his every gesture with innate style.

He might have inherited his father's looks, but his mother's aristocratic genes showed in his bearing, in his manner. Underneath that sometimes surly exterior lurked the heart and soul of a gentleman. She had only to look around his home to recognize his inborn good taste.

"My mother's all that, and then some," he said, reaching over to pour more wine into her glass. "And now let's talk about you. Do you have any other siblings besides your sister?"

"No."

"Which of you came first?"

"I did, by six years."

"Making her about twenty."

"Twenty-two."

"In other words, plenty old enough to have developed the smarts to steer clear of a man so rotten inside that he'd steal her baby."

Linda's hackles, temporarily soothed by that brief glimpse of his more human side, rose again in defense. "I no more like it when you pass judgment on my sister without knowing the first thing about her, than you did when I presumed to criticize your mother."

"But I do know something about her," he said, unruffled. "I know she's an unmarried mother, and her relationship with the father didn't pan out. She was probably spoiled as a child and never got over being the baby of the family. When things went sour with the boyfriend, she probably moved back home to be looked after by good old mom and dad."

"And how do you arrive at those conclusions?"

"When I'm faced with a situation in which the mother of a missing child *isn't* the one raising hell and putting a lid on it, there are only two conclusions I'm likely to reach. Either she doesn't care, or she's the passive, helpless kind who leaves it to someone else to go to bat for her." He shrugged and raised both hands, palms up. "It doesn't take a genius to figure that out, now does it?"

Galled by his arrogance and the fact that, in June's case at least and with very few facts to go on, he'd profiled her with uncanny accuracy, Linda said, "How fortunate you must feel, to be so blessed!"

"No. I'm smart enough to pick up the signs, that's all. Take you, for example."

"I'd rather you didn't," she said, uncomfortable at the idea of being the subject of his too-perceptive analysis.

His smile sent goose bumps racing the length of her spine. "Figuratively speaking only, cookie, so relax. You're not my type, although—" he tilted his head to one side and surveyed her through narrowed eyes "—under different circumstances, it's conceivable that I might find you satisfactory."

Satisfactory? She almost choked on a mushroom!

"Would you like some water?" he inquired, starting up from his chair with phony concern. "Or is the Heimlich maneuver called for?"

"Keep your hands to yourself!" she spat, wiping her eyes with the corner of her napkin. "And just for the record, you're not my type, either."

"No?" He sat down again, amusement tugging at the corners of his mouth. "Time will tell. Meanwhile, getting back to our discussion, you're the complete opposite of your sister. Proactive, stubborn, impulsive."

"How you do you figure that?"

"You're here, aren't you, and going to extraordinary lengths to persuade me to help you, despite my less than encouraging response?"

"I'd say that's pretty self-evident."

"Yet I doubt, if it were *your* child that was missing, your sister would be sitting across the table from me now— mostly because you wouldn't dream of entrusting someone else with the task, but also because she wouldn't have the stomach for the job. She's probably very good at weeping, wringing her hands, and drumming up sympathy, but basically useless in any sort of crisis. You, on the other hand, rush in where the proverbial angels fear to tread—without any sort of backup provision in place, should your first course of action fail." He took a sip of wine and regarded her quizzically. "Well, how am I doing so far?"

She'd have lied if there'd been any point in it. Instead she watered down the truth. "Quite well, I suppose."

"And that's it?" He raised his brows in feigned surprise. "You're not going to lambaste me for saying mean and nasty things about your poor, misunderstood sister? Have a tantrum and throw your plate across the room, maybe? What's the matter, Linda? Didn't your dinner agree with you?"

"I wouldn't dream of abusing such beautiful china," she

said, striving for nonchalance. "Did you inherit it from your grandmother, as well?"

"Yes," he said. "And stop trying to sidestep the question. How close to the mark am I with your sister?"

"Too close. Bull's-eye close." Defeated, she pushed aside her plate. "You're right. June isn't strong like me. She's a gentle, passive soul who hates confrontations of any kind—which just goes to show how bad things must have been between her and Kirk that she'd walk out on him when she was expecting his baby."

"What's your impression of this Kirk?"

"Only what I've been told about him. She met him while I was in Europe. I've seen photos of him and know that he's American, appears to have money and works in the computer field, but I've never actually met him or spoken to him in person."

"You're not going to be much help tracking him down then, are you?"

"No, Mr. Sullivan," she said, folding her hands meekly. "That's why I'm throwing myself on your mercy."

"You'll stand a better chance of getting it if you dispense with the annoying 'Mr. Sullivan'. My name's Mac."

"I'll try to remember that, just as I'm sure you'll remember I'm Linda, the next time you get the urge to call me to heel."

A scowl marred his handsome brow. "I bet you're a nurse when you're not on a mission. You look like the type who'd enjoy wreaking vengeance on a guy by stabbing a foot-long needle in his behind when he's at your mercy."

"Sorry to disappoint you, but this time your fabled instincts are way off target. I'm not a nurse—but I am very handy with a knife, which you might want to remember. My sister might be guilty of bad judgment, but that's her only sin, and I won't sit idly by while you rip her character to shreds."

"You can't afford to be overly protective of her, either. If I'm to be of any use at all, I need to know everything about her—the flaws and weaknesses, as well as the strengths. And I don't mind telling you, right now I don't see a whole lot of strengths.''

He was hard. Inflexible. She saw it in the set of his jaw, the flat, cold light in his eyes. He wouldn't have much patience with a woman like June. ''Haven't you ever made a mistake about someone—in a personal context, I mean?''

''Sure,'' he said without a flicker of regret or emotion. ''I made a huge mistake thinking police work and marriage went together.''

''You're married?'' The possibility struck a blow she'd never have anticipated. He seemed so self-reliant; so...*single*. And yet, was it really likely a man like this wouldn't have a wife—or at least, a woman?

''Not anymore.'' His smile struck her as uncommonly fond.

''Do you still care about your ex-wife?''

''Sure I still care. Why wouldn't I?''

''Because, as you just said, you're divorced.''

''That doesn't automatically make her the villain of the piece. The marriage is what didn't work, and it wouldn't say much for my judgment if I chose an outright bitch to be my wife.''

''Are you still in touch with each other?''

''Occasionally. We call each other on birthdays and Christmas—things like that. She checks up on me to make sure I'm not hibernating too long at a stretch. I give her the benefit of my unasked-for advice on the men in her life, take her to lunch when I find myself on her stamping ground.''

''That's beyond my understanding,'' Linda said, marveling at his sanguine outlook. ''In my experience, divorce is synonymous with...all the bad things in life.''

Mac surveyed her curiously. ''Exactly what is your experience in this field?''

''My parents divorced when I was in my teens. We

haven't heard from my father in years. Are you and your ex-wife still lovers?''

She couldn't believe she'd actually come out and asked such a question, and would have given anything to withdraw it. He wasn't impressed by it, either. ''What's it to you, cookie? I thought you came here to enlist my help, not quiz me about my sexual history. Are you done with that plate?''

''Yes, thank you,'' she mumbled, still awash in embarrassment. ''Dinner was delicious.''

''Nice of you to say so. Did I mention, when we went over the house rules, that the one who doesn't cook gets to clean up once the meal's over?''

''You seem to live by a great many rules.''

''I make them up as I go along, especially when I'm saddled with uninvited houseguests.''

''Well, it's easy enough to be rid of me,'' she said, rallying. ''All you have to do is agree to help me find my niece, and I'll leave.''

''And if I don't?''

''I won't budge.''

''Then it seems I'm stuck with you either way, since you don't have any other place to stay tonight.''

Either way? A flicker of hope took hold of her. ''Does that mean you're prepared to take on the case?''

Face unreadable, he swirled the wine in his glass and took his time replying. ''It means I'm prepared to consider it. Not, I hasten to add, because I find your powers of persuasion irresistible or because your sister was fool enough to get herself pregnant by a man she didn't know well enough to trust, but because a young and helpless child is the ultimate victim.''

''Oh, thank you!'' she exclaimed, relief leaving her voice shaking with emotion. ''Thank you so much, Mac! You don't know how grateful I am, or what this will mean to my family. Now, probably the best place to start—''

He cut her off with a decisive gesture, slicing his hand

through the air like an ax blade and thumping it down on the table so hard that the plates rattled and the wine danced in the glasses. "Let's get something straight right off," he said. "*If* I take this on, *I* will be the one to decide on the best place to start. *I* will be the one who calls the shots. Not you, and not your family. With all due respect to your understandable concern, you are not the ones with the experience or contacts needed to bring that baby back home. But only, as I said, *if* I decide to pursue the case, something which is by no means certain."

"What do I have to do to clinch things in my favor?"

He smiled. A dazzling, beautiful smile, which should have reassured her but which inspired instead the tingling sense that accepting favors from him would come with a very high price—one she might never be able to afford. "I'll let you know when I've figured it out, cookie," he said, rising from his seat and strolling languidly to the couch at the other end of the room. "Meanwhile, tackle the dishes."

CHAPTER THREE

LULLED by the crackle of the flames in the hearth, and the muted clatter coming from the kitchen, Mac stretched out his legs and, leaning his head on the back of the couch, contemplated the high cathedral ceiling, and the ramifications of his decision.

He was going to take the case. Not because he liked her—which he did. Not because she was a firebrand and he found himself responding to her energy. And not because of the spark of sexual awareness, which he'd denied to her but which, reluctantly, he admitted to himself. They were the worst reasons in the world to get involved, especially with a situation which promised to be messy at best.

That he might be powerless to repair things also did not escape him. God knew, he didn't need another infant tragedy on his résumé. One was more than enough.

But maybe...*maybe*...by returning this missing baby, safe and alive, to her mother's arms, he might lay the ghost of that other one. Might at last shed the guilt which still haunted his dreams, three years later.

And if he failed a second time?

He closed his eyes, as if by doing so, he could blot out any such possibility. And right away, the same old images, the same old sounds, filled his mind. The cold dread of premonition he'd known before he even opened the trunk of the abandoned car crawled over him again. He saw the pale blue blanket, the tiny foot. Tasted the bitter pill of rage mixed with helplessness. Heard the mother's wrenching sobs echoing from an empty nursery, the shuddering heartbreak in the father's voice.

"Are you sleeping?"

She startled him, stepping softly to where he sprawled on the couch, but he took care not to let it show. Already, the old instinct to reveal nothing of himself, while at the same time gleaning everything from those around him, had clicked into action.

"With all the racket you're making?" he said, easing himself upright with deceptive indolence. "Hardly! I was trying to decide if I should let you sleep in your car, as you so rashly threatened to do, or if I should play the gentleman and offer you my bed—without me in it, of course."

She stood beside the coffee table, a dish towel tied around her waist. "You'll play the gentleman," she said, her smile disturbingly sweet. "Of course."

"What makes you so sure?"

"I've got you figured out."

"Don't try to second-guess me, cookie. I'm not that easy to read. And don't tell me you've finished cleaning up the kitchen already."

"Down to the very last spoon," she said. "Would you like to inspect?"

"I'll take your word for it. Do you know how to make a decent pot of coffee?"

"I can try," she said, docile as a lamb. "Provided you give me instructions."

"Eight measures of extra-fine grind to six cups of water. Coffee's in the freezer, coffeemaker on the counter next to the sink. And use filtered water."

"Cream with it?"

"Black."

"Very good, sir." She bobbed a curtsy, holding out the dish towel like a crinoline. "Anything else?"

"Yes," he said. "Disappear and get on with it before I change my mind and show you the door. You're beginning to irritate the hell out of me."

With another bobbing curtsy, she scuttled off. A log rolled dangerously close to the front of the hearth, shooting sparks in all directions. Lunging to his feet, he toed it back in place and added another chunk of fir to keep it anchored. Then, since he was up anyway, he went to the liquor cabinet and selected a bottle of Courvoisier, lured to indulge himself by the rich aroma of espresso filtering from the kitchen.

"At least you're good for something," he acknowledged, tasting the contents of the demitasse she passed to him a few minutes later. "Will you join me in a brandy?"

"Thank you, yes. But just a small one. It's been a very long day and I don't want to pass out on you again."

He poured an inch into a snifter and gave it to her. "I've been going over a few things in my mind," he said, running his fingertips over his jaw.

She sat motionless at the other end of the couch, the snifter held between her hands, her eyes huge in her face. Unusual color, those eyes. Strangely clear, like blue topaz, and made all the more arresting by her long, dark lashes.

"Are you a natural blond?" he inquired.

Her mouth fell open. "That's what you've been sitting here thinking about?"

"No. It just occurred to me to wonder."

"I'm a natural blond. Would it matter if I wasn't?"

"Not a bit." He took a mouthful of the brandy and rolled it around his palate. Good stuff, Courvoisier. Fine way to end a meal. "You can still sleep in my bed tonight. Alone, since you're not my type."

"Praise the Lord!"

"And I'll help you find your missing niece."

At that, the sassy starch went out of her. She sagged against the sofa cushions, her relief manifest. "If you do that," she said, "there's nothing I won't do for you in return."

"Be careful what you promise."

"I mean it," she insisted, her eyes shining with unshed tears. "*Anything* I can do for you, just ask."

"For now, a refill on the coffee will suffice. Consider it a down payment."

Her hand shook slightly as she poured, but she kept her

tears in check. "We should discuss financial arrangements," she said, obviously focusing on the practical to avoid giving in to the emotional.

"Money isn't an issue. I'm taking on this crusade for personal reasons."

"Nevertheless, if there are expenses, I'm the one who should pay them."

"Whatever." He shrugged. "We'll start in the morning, when you're more rested. But be warned: you'll have to be patient. I'm no miracle worker. This might take some time."

Her face fell. "Oh, I hope not, Mac! It's been seven weeks already. Kirk Thayer could be anywhere by now."

"And hopefully feeling secure enough that he's stopped running." Against his better judgment, he reached for her hand. It felt small and warm and soft in his. Like a curled up flower. "If we're going to work together on this, you're going to have to trust me, cookie."

The tears glimmered again. "I know," she said, barely above a whisper.

"And I'm not offering any guarantees. Remember that."

"I will." She sniffed delicately. "If you're really going to let me stay here tonight, I should bring in my bag from the car."

"I'll change the bed linen while you do that."

"No, please don't. I can sleep perfectly well on the couch."

"I'll change the bed linen," he repeated, emphasizing each word distinctly.

She backed off at once. "Yes. All right. Whatever you say. And thank you."

"Quit thanking me. Once is enough." He removed her untouched drink and set it on the coffee table. "Go get your stuff."

She made it as far as the front door, then stopped and looked back at him, uncertainty in every line of her slender body. "Mac? You won't change your mind and lock me out?"

"I don't go back on my word," he told her curtly, refusing to let her vulnerability touch him. "I'll open the garage for you. Bring your car down and park it with mine, then come in through the side door next to the laundry room."

The wind had dropped. Above the tall evergreens edging the side of his driveway, a million stars spattered the sky. The roar of the surf had died to a low murmur, which rolled through the otherwise quiet night like a lullaby.

Before climbing into her car, she stopped and inhaled deeply, letting the cold, clean air fill her lungs and sweep her soul with relief. He was going to help her, and even though he'd said he might not succeed, she knew that he would. He was that kind of man.

A personal crusade, he'd called it, which described perfectly what he'd promised to undertake because, in her view, he was a modern-day knight. Brave, fearless, honorable—and driven. He would allow nothing to come between him and his objective. She knew that, too. With absolute certainty.

As promised, he'd raised the doors to the big triple garage. The space between his massive four-wheel-drive truck and sleek Jaguar convertible was just wide enough for her to slide her little two-seater hatchback between them.

"I checked the kitchen and you do good work," he told her, when she let herself into the house again. "Keeping you around might turn out to be a smarter move than I first thought."

"I can't imagine why you'd want anyone staying here, if it means you have to move out of your bedroom," she said, noting the quilt and extra pillows he'd piled on the fireside chair. "It bothers me that I'm inconveniencing you like this."

"I've survived a lot worse than sleeping on an eight-foot-long couch,'' he said. ''This is nothing compared to spending the night on a stakeout in an unmarked patrol car. And what makes you think I necessarily sleep alone every time I have a houseguest? How do you know tonight's not the exception to the rule?''

She didn't, any more than she needed to be reminded he was no monk. One glance into those eyes, at that mouth, was enough to feel the simmering sensuality of the man. ''I'm sure you have your share of female admirers,'' she said, sounding as stiff-necked as a dried-up old schoolmarm.

''Don't pout,'' he ordered. ''And don't try to tell me you haven't shared your bed with some guy or other before now. No normal woman gets to be twenty-eight these days, and still be as sexually innocent as the day she was born.''

''Well, I guess that puts me in my place, then,'' she said. ''Color me not normal and glad of it!''

He stopped in the process of spreading the quilt over the cushions and flung her an astonished stare. ''You're kidding me, right?''

''Wrong! As wrong as your outdated notion that today's woman can't wait to leap into bed with the first man who crosses her path. Quite a lot of us prefer to wait until the *right* man shows up.''

''Hold out for marriage, you mean?''

''Yes,'' she said, deciding he didn't need to know that the only reason she remained a virgin was by default. ''Do you have a problem with that?''

''Theoretically not,'' he replied, beaming cheerfully. ''But in practice, I have to say I prefer—''

She had no wish to hear. Bad enough that his grin left her weak at the knees, without having him make further inroads on her moral fortitude. She hadn't defended her virginity against Alberto Tartaglia's failed seduction to surrender it now to someone who found it laughably outdated. ''Never mind! It's none of my business.''

''Not interested, huh?''

"Not in the least. The only thing I care about right now is a hot bath and getting some sleep, so if you'll show me where—"

"Down there." He pointed to a curving stairwell. "You can't miss it."

Indeed not! Rather than the conventional arrangement found in other homes, his bedroom was a mirror image of the main story; a wide, spacious open area, with one entire wall of windows facing the sea, and a king-size bed positioned in the middle of the floor so that its occupant could look out at the view.

The only difference was that, whereas the kitchen was separated from the more formal living and dining areas by an open archway on the main floor, the en suite bathroom attached to his bedroom did at least offer the privacy of a door.

Laying her open suitcase on a bench at the foot of the bed, she took out her toiletries, a nightgown, and a light cotton robe. He'd left clean towels folded on the deck of the big soaker tub, a bar of soap, and half a jar of expensive bath crystals. Not his, she was sure—he didn't strike her as the type to wallow in gardenia-scented water—which probably meant they belonged to one of his lady loves.

"Thanks, but no thanks!" she muttered, and decided to take a shower instead. It seemed altogether less intimate. And keeping her association with him strictly impersonal, she decided, as the hot water streamed over her travel-weary body, was the only sensible route to take. It made everything so much less complicated.

Yet for all that she'd put in a sixteen-hour day, and a good part of it spent driving at that, when at last she crawled into bed, she was too restless to sleep. The strange house, its disturbingly attractive owner, the possibility that, before much longer, June might have her baby back—these thoughts kept her mind active long after her body had nested under the goose down quilt and snuggled into luxurious relaxation.

Finally, after long minutes of tossing and turning, she flung aside the covers, switched on the lamp again and, desperate for something to divert her, pulled open the drawer in the bedside table. Surely he kept a paperback handy for those nights when insomnia struck?

In fact, she found two: one a science fiction novel, which definitely was not to her taste, and the other a law enforcement manual of some sort which looked equally uninteresting. But tucked between them were several sheets of single-spaced manuscript whose headers indicated plainly enough that they were part of the book Melissa had told her he was writing.

Of course, she had no business reading them. No business foraging through his drawers to begin with, come to that. But the paper leaped into her hands as if she had magnets attached to the tips of her fingers, and for all that she tried to resist, the words swam into focus before her eyes, horrifying and compelling.

Immediately drawn into a world inhabited by people whose capacity for evil so far exceeded anything she could imagine, she paid no attention to the peripheral sound of him moving around on the floor above her, and so remained quite unaware that he was coming down the stairs until his shadow, grotesquely elongated in the lamplight, swam across the ceiling. Then, in a flurry of agitation, she tried to cover up her actions.

It was not to be. Although she managed to stuff the papers back where she'd found them, the spine of the manual became wedged as she went to slide the drawer shut, thereby preventing it from closing. Desperate, she grasped the book by the cover and attempted to pull it loose, praying it wouldn't tear.

It did not. It flew free and in doing so, dislodged an open packet whose contents, individually wrapped in shiny foil, spilled into her lap like so many priceless gold coins.

Appalled, she clapped a hand to her mouth and stared at

them, willing them to disappear and take her with them. "Oh, my stars!" she mouthed, under her breath.

"No, my dear, they're condoms," Mac Sullivan said, leaning on the head rail and letting his voice drift over her in waves of irony. "They're used for contraception—preventing babies, to innocents like you who probably think contraception's a dirty word. And in case you don't know how they work, men wear them over their—"

"I know what they are and how they're used!" she squeaked, practically delirious with embarrassment. "I'm a virgin, not an illiterate nincompoop!"

"You're all that and then some," he advised her, abandoning his vantage point and coming around the bed to confront her. "Tell me, cookie, were you planning to sneak up on me while I slept, and try one on me for size?"

"Certainly not!" she said, sounding more like a deranged mouse with every syllable she uttered.

"Then what were you doing?"

The question held none of his earlier banter, any more than his eyes, fixed on her with laserlike intent, held so much as a glint of humor. Dearly though she would have liked to look away, she found her gaze imprisoned by his. "I couldn't sleep," she confessed. "I was looking for something to read."

He reached into the still-open drawer to where the manuscript pages lay in conspicuous disarray. "'Something' being this?"

She didn't have to admit to the sin. Guilt painting her face a flaming red spoke for itself.

"Do you listen in on phone calls, as well?" he inquired coldly. "Intercept incoming e-mail? Steal? Should I keep everything under lock and key while you're a guest in my house? Sleep with a gun under my pillow?"

"No," she said in a shaken voice, pulling the quilt up to her chin as if it could protect her from the chill of his displeasure. "Stop blowing everything out of proportion. I'm not a criminal."

"How do I know that? How do I know you didn't make up this whole story about a missing baby, just to get past my front door and snoop through things which are none of your business?"

"Oh, please! Stop being so paranoid! All I did was pick up a few typewritten pages. I didn't even have time to read any of them before you caught me, for heaven's sake, and I won't touch them again."

"No, you won't," he said, tucking them under his arm. "I'll make sure of that."

That he was furious yet remained utterly in control was enough for her to glimpse the steely sense of purpose from which he drew much of his strength. This was how he must have been during his detective days, she thought with an inward shiver. Merciless. Relentless.

She would far rather have him on her side, than against her.

But recognizing that didn't stop her from putting to him a question she surely had the right to ask. "Why did you come down here to begin with? Were you spying on me?"

"Now who's being paranoid?" he shot back. "I heard you messing around in the drawer and figured the moonlight was keeping you awake and you were looking for the remote control, which operates the electronic blinds. So, like the good host I'm trying hard to be, I came down to give you a hand."

"I didn't notice any remote control doohickey in the drawer."

"Naturally not. You were too busy playing with my condoms and reading material not meant for your eyes." He yanked the drawer more fully open and withdrew the gadget in question. "This," he said, slapping it down on the nightstand, "you may play with to your heart's content. Kindly keep your cotton-picking chicken pluckers off everything else!"

He stamped off, leaving her too cowed to ask if he had a book she could borrow. Better to lie there wide-awake for the rest of the night, than risk ticking him off any more than she already had. And yet, there was something very comforting and solid about his presence. Not much escaped him, nor did he tolerate fools easily. And although they were qualities which she found disconcerting when directed at her, instinct told her they'd prove very useful in the search for June's baby.

Surprisingly she fell asleep soon after, and didn't stir until the bright light of morning glinting off the sea speared her eyelids just after seven the next day.

There was no sound from above. Moving quietly so as not to disturb him, she brushed her teeth and washed her face, ran a brush through her hair and dressed in a blue fleece jogging suit. Then, carrying her running shoes, she crept up the stairs, intending to slip out of the house and go for a walk along the beach until he was up and about.

They hadn't parted on the best of terms, last night. She didn't want to incur his further wrath by waking him before he was ready to face the day.

She'd reached the bottom of the cliff steps when he suddenly appeared atop the sand dune directly in front of her. Towel flung over his shoulders, black swimming trunks clinging to his hips, and water dripping from his hair, he stood silhouetted against the sky like some proud sea god washed ashore by an errant wave.

"So you're up finally," he said, bounding down to meet her with a surefooted agility she envied. It had taken more skill than she'd expected when she'd scaled the dunes the day before, and twice she'd gone sprawling as the deep, flour-soft sand gave way beneath her feet. "You were still out cold when I came downstairs."

"You were in my bedroom?" An uneasy thrill shot through her at the idea that he'd watched her sleeping. She'd never been the kind who, once she closed her eyes, was so dead to the world that nothing disturbed her. *You'd know if a cat walked over the lawn,* her father had once said, when she was about eight and had awoken in the middle of the night, sure she could hear something moving outside her window.

"No," Mac Sullivan said. "I was in mine. I keep my clothes and stuff down there and figured I'd better wear trunks today, with you likely to faint dead away if you happened to catch sight of me buck naked."

"You might as well not have bothered," she said, unable to help noticing the stunning fidelity with which the wet fabric of his swimsuit followed the contours of his pelvis.

"Then don't look—unless, of course, you can't tear your fascinated gaze away."

"Dream on!" she retorted, aiming for haughty indifference but managing to sound only as if she were slightly asthmatic. No man had the right to look so perfect regardless of what he was or wasn't wearing. "I've got bigger things on my mind than anything you might want to show off!"

She didn't need his sudden brilliant smile to tell her he'd caught the unintentional innuendo in her words. "Perhaps you should rephrase that," he informed her. "Otherwise, I might be tempted to show you how wrong you are."

They'd spent no more than a couple of minutes together, and already her resolve to keep the peace was wearing thin. Restraining herself with an effort, she said, "Let's start over again. Good morning, Mr. Sullivan. Did you have a nice swim?"

"I had a bloody cold swim. If you had a grain of pity in your soul, you'd offer to make me a nice hot breakfast."

"I'll be happy to do that. I'd have started on it already, if I hadn't been afraid of presuming too heavily on your hospitality. A man's kitchen, at least in this instance, is his castle."

"I can always use a handmaiden. Feel free to make yourself useful while I shower, then we'll go over strategies while we eat."

His refrigerator was well stocked, yielding everything she needed to put together a meal guaranteed to please even his discerning palate. By the time he came back upstairs, brief-case in hand, she had fresh-squeezed orange juice and coffee waiting on the patio table, and fresh-from-the-oven cornmeal muffins, pear preserves, and a blue cheese omelet garnished with Ribier grapes and kiwi fruit ready to serve.

"Well," he said, eyeing the plate she placed in front of him, "I must admit, I'm impressed. Where'd you learn to cook like this?"

"Oh, here and there," she said airily. "I've been known to turn out an acceptable dish or two in my time."

He sampled the omelet appreciatively. "No kidding! We've got more in common than I'd have guessed. I just might let you help me with dinner."

"Dinner?" She set down her coffee cup and regarded him with dismay, neither his compliment nor its unwitting irony impressed her nearly as much as the suggestion that they'd be spending another day there at his house. "But I thought we were going to start the search this morning?"

"We are," he said, slathering butter on a muffin.

"We won't get far if we're still here this evening!"

"Patience, cookie," he counseled idly. "Cases don't get solved by people running off half-cocked. Until we have some clue as to where Thayer might have gone, we stay put."

"But—!"

"We stay put, Linda. Here, where my contacts can reach me." The lazy drawl was gone, eclipsed by the tough, un-yielding tone she'd heard the night before. "We do this my way."

"And I don't have any say at all in *how?*"

"I laid down my terms very clearly last night and you didn't seem to have a problem with them then. If, however, you've changed your mind in the interim, feel free to hit the road and go it alone."

"No," she said hastily. "We'll do it your way."

He removed a notepad and pen from the briefcase. "Okay, let's get started. I'm going to question you at length. I want you to answer me as fully and truthfully as possible.''

"What kind of questions?"

"Background information, mainly. Begin by telling me how your sister met Thayer."

"They worked in the same building."

"Same company?"

"No. Not even on the same floor. They met in the elevator one day when it was pouring with rain, and shared a taxi to the airport. He was leaving on vacation, and she was meeting a friend flying in from down east. A few weeks later, she ran into him again, he invited her out, and that's how it began.''

"Do you know the name of the company he worked for?''

"No. But all it'll take is a phone call home to find out."

"Fine. We'll put that at the top of your list of things to do, once we're finished here. As soon as we've got a name, I'll call in a few favors and get someone up in Washington to have him checked out. Vancouver's not that large a city, so it shouldn't take long.''

"But we're not from *that* Vancouver," she exclaimed, realizing they were talking at cross-purposes. "We live in the one in British Columbia.''

He stopped writing and stared at her incredulously. "Are you telling me you're from Canada?''

"Yes.''

"And that's where your niece was born?''

"Well…yes. Is there something wrong with that?''

"Only if you think my not having a single contact north of the border is a problem! Why the devil didn't you say something before now? And why come to me for help, when you could have turned to the Mounties whose major claim to fame is that they always get their man?''

"First, you didn't ask. Second, the RCMP's involvement came to a grinding halt the day they found out Kirk had skipped the country. And third, his movements were traced as far as Portland, which conveniently happens to be in Oregon where you also live.''

''Linda...!'' He leaned his elbow on the table and slapped the heel of his hand to his forehead.

''What?'' she cried. ''Don't tell me this makes a difference and you've changed your mind about helping me!''

''It makes a difference,'' he said. ''For a start, even if the Vancouver police contacted the Portland police—''

''They did! I know that for a fact.''

''Even so,'' he said, ''the most the Portland PD would do is file the report. Honey, I don't know how to tell you this, but hundreds of children go missing every year, and once it's established they've been taken out of state, let alone out of the country, finding them becomes...''

''Impossible?'' She shook her head furiously. ''No! Don't even try telling me that, because I won't accept it. You've done it yourself. Often. Everyone knows that. You've found people who didn't want to be found. You've brought families together again.''

She didn't know exactly when she started crying, but she knew precisely why. She was frightened that he was going to back out of their deal and she'd be returning to Vancouver with nothing to show for her efforts. Petrified that if Angela wasn't found soon, June would never be the same again. Horribly afraid that if things dragged on much longer, she'd end up burying her mother.

''Hey!'' He shoved back his chair and came around the table to where she sat, weeping helplessly. Hopelessly. *''Hey!''*

He pulled her up and held her against him. Wrapped his strong, beautiful arms around her and pressed her head into the angle of his broad, capable shoulder. Crooned that name she hated—*cookie!*—over and over again in her ear. Stroked his long, tanned fingers through her hair and down her neck. And when none of that stemmed the tears, he turned her face up to his and kissed her.

It should not have happened like that, at a moment sodden with despair. Nothing so exquisitely bestowed deserved to be touched with the kind of grief she felt at that moment—exquisite not because it possessed all the seductive fire and fury of which she knew he was capable, but because of the gentleness he brought to bear on the moment. Because of the compassion.

His lips lingered, firm and cool. Healing where they touched. Spreading a sense of calm that permeated her entire being until, at last, she could raise her eyes to his and say, "What comes next, Mac?"

He stroked his finger down her cheek. Almost sighed, and instead blew out a long, unsteady breath that breezed sweetly over her face. "I'm taking you home," he said.

CHAPTER FOUR

SHE jerked away from him, swiping the back of her hand over her mouth as if she'd just tasted something vile. "Oh, silly me, to have thought that was a kiss, when it was really the big kiss-off! Well, I'm not leaving here, and you can't make me!"

Part of him wanted to laugh; another part to turn her reaction into an opportunity to wash his hands of the whole affair. But neither equaled the reeling impact of having held her in his arms and sampled her mouth.

It was only a kiss, for Pete's sake, and not even an exotic one at that! He'd kissed other women at much greater length and with a much more seductive goal in mind—but reaped less than one-tenth the stimulation he'd found in that brief exchange with her.

Aiming to counteract her effect on him, he said, "Are you always this childish when you think you've been thwarted?"

"Childish?" Her eyes were swimming again, but he refused to be swayed by the fact. One mistake a day was all he allowed himself. "How about 'foolish' for ever having believed I could count on you?"

"And what have I said to make you think you can't?"

Her laugh edged a bit too close to hysteria for his liking. "Your threatening to send me home doesn't exactly inspire confidence in your so-called commitment to my cause."

"Your inability to understand plain English doesn't fill me with elation, either," he said sharply. "I did not threaten to send you home, I said I was going to *take* you home. Recognize the difference."

That stopped her in midtirade. "You're...coming with me?"

"You've got it, cookie."

"Why?"

"I want to talk to the people who knew this Kirk Thayer. If I'm going to run him to earth, I need to find out everything there is to know about him." He gestured to the remains of their breakfast. "Clean up here and get yourself organized, while I throw some things in a suitcase and make a couple of phone calls. I want to be on the road within the hour."

She bristled, as he half expected she would. "You must have mistaken me for a police dog, trained to obey your every command."

"No chance of that ever happening," he said, heading inside the house. "You don't have the brains for the job."

Her reply floated after him: a three word suggestion, succinct and unmistakable in its meaning.

"That's anatomically impossible, even for me," he called out, taking the stairs two at a time to his office on the third floor. "And shame on you for resorting to language that would make a stevedore blush."

They set off forty-five minutes later. "I thought about flying up to Vancouver," he said, cruising north along the scenic coast road, just slightly above the speed limit, "but with all the hanging around and jumping through hoops it involves, we can be there almost as fast by driving."

"I doubt that. It took me two days to get to your place."

"Given the kind of car you drive, plus the fact that you were probably poking along at forty miles an hour, that doesn't surprise me."

The turnoff for the highway linking the coast road to the Interstate lay a couple of hundred yards ahead. Taking the exit ramp at a fair clip, he filtered into the mainstream traffic, steered past a couple of semis, and pulled into the passing lane.

"I, on the other hand," he said, stepping on the gas and enjoying her stifled gasp of alarm as the Jaguar, responsive to his slightest touch, leaped forward, "prefer to get to where I'm going with all due speed."

"I prefer to arrive alive, if you don't mind!"

"Relax, Linda," he said, patting her knee. "I'll get you there in one piece, I promise."

"And then what?"

"We'll do some nosing around. Check with the RCMP to see if anything new's turned up. Talk to people who knew Thayer. Learn what we can about his background, habits, things like that."

"By people, I hope you don't mean June. She's pretty fragile right now."

"I mean anybody who might shed some light on his actions," he said flatly. "June, your mother, Thayer's neighbors, colleagues, friends. We've got to start somewhere, yes?"

"I suppose so." She stared at her clenched hands gloomily.

"You're not exactly brimming over with enthusiasm. Why is that, I wonder?"

"I feel I'm running in circles and getting nowhere. I spent two whole days driving from Vancouver to Trillium Cove, and here we are, spending another whole day driving back again."

He swung another glance at her. With the top down on the car, the wind was having a heyday with her hair. In marked contrast to her otherwise troubled demeanor, it streamed around her face, carefree and wild.

Squashing the crazy urge to reach out and feel its pale, corn-silk texture sliding through his fingers, he said, "You could have saved yourself the trip if you'd called me first, you know."

"Even if I'd been able to get hold of your phone number, would you have spoken to me? Agreed to help me?"

"Probably not," he admitted ruefully.

He could, and did, hang up on importuning phone calls from strangers; disregard their messages on his voice mail. But even he, hardened case that he'd become, hadn't been able to turn his back on a woman whose physical presence defined the weary hopelessness hers had betrayed.

"That's why I had to come to see you in person."

He drummed his fingers on the leather-bound steering wheel and debated broaching the one subject which had been nagging at the back of his mind ever since he'd agreed to take on the case. "How much do you really know about me, Linda?"

"Only what I've read, what my journalist friend mentioned, and what you yourself have told me. I know you've already published one book, which is being heralded as the closest thing to a bible ever to land on a police chief's desk, and you're working on a second. That you do some media work once in a very rare while, and occasionally get called in to consult when an official investigation hits a snag. You're also difficult, reclusive and guard your privacy as if it were on a par with the Hope diamond." A thread of laughter lightened her voice. "I half expected I'd find myself looking down the barrel of a shotgun when you caught me trespassing on your territory yesterday."

"Yet you hung around anyway, even after I told you to take a hike."

"Yes. With my sister practically catatonic, and my niece missing nearly two months, what did I have to lose?"

He didn't tell her, *Quite possibly the only thing you have left, which is hope!* If they were chasing a lost cause, she'd find out soon enough. Instead he said, "Do you know why I turned in my badge?"

"Because you're a rebel and wouldn't play by the rules."

"No," he said. "Because I screwed up the last case I worked on and a child died as a result. A baby, Linda, not much older than your niece."

She recoiled, burying herself deeper into the plush leather

seat. "But it wasn't really your fault. You were hamstrung by protocol."

"*It was my fault.* I was the one who undertook to bring that child home, and I was the one who failed."

"Why are you telling me this now?" she asked, in a small, wounded voice.

"Because I'm no miracle worker. I can't guarantee I'm going to find your sister's baby. I can't promise you anything except that I'll do my best. I don't want to mislead you on that. And I don't want you misleading yourself. So if, in light of what I've just said, you don't think I'm the right man for the job after all, feel free to say so. I'll drive you to the nearest airport, put you on a plane for Vancouver, arrange to have your car delivered to you within the week, and no hard feelings either way."

The silence spun out, matching the miles. Finally, when he was about ready to stop the car and shake her into responding, she said, "I'm not going to change my mind. I...trust you."

"So did the parents of that other baby, and I let them down."

"So you say. But if Angela..." Her voice quivered and died. Obviously fighting to bring her emotions under control, she drew in a long, shaking breath and tried again. "If something's happened to my niece and we're too late to save her, I need to know it wasn't because of lack of effort on my part. I need to know I gave it my best shot—which, at this point, is you. Otherwise, I don't think I'll be able to face my family ever again."

"You took a real chance, just showing up on my doorstep like that, you know," he said, steering the conversation into a less sensitive vein. "What if I'd been away or refused to see you?"

"I wouldn't let myself dwell on those possibilities. I had to take some sort of action. *Anything* was better than sitting at home waiting for the phone to ring, and being afraid to answer because the news might be bad."

"Are you always this impetuous?"

"Only if the occasion calls for it. Why? Haven't you ever done something on impulse?"

"Yeah," he said. "I got married on one."

"Why didn't things work out, do you suppose?"

"I was too obsessed with my work. I brought it home with me. It was my mistress, always coming between us, even in the bedroom." He swung a glance at her, deeming it wise to make his next point, even though their association was purely professional. Women sometimes got strange ideas on the strength of very little. "I'm not good marriage material, cookie."

She turned to watch the passing scene so that he couldn't read her face, and said, "Were they your ex-wife's bath crystals I saw in your bathroom?"

"No. She's never seen my house. Never set foot in Trillium Cove, as far as I know. She'd be bored silly in a place like that. She's a city woman, born and bred."

"Do you miss her?"

She was beginning to irritate the hell out of him again. It seemed to be something she did very easily, when she put her mind to it. "Sometimes I miss the sharing, the closeness. But I've learned to compensate. A man doesn't have to take a wife to find companionship, if you get my drift."

That pretty much killed the conversation until they approached the outskirts of Salem where they stopped for a sandwich. "Not up to your omelet standard, by any means," he told her, inspecting the sparse layers of his pastrami on rye. "Where'd you learn to cook like that anyway, at the Cordon Bleu in Paris?"

"Among other places, yes."

He gulped and just about swallowed his sandwich whole. "You're kidding, right?"

"No." She picked daintily at the shredded lettuce hanging over the edge of her chicken salad on whole wheat. "I spent eighteen months at the New York Restaurant School, followed that with nine months in Paris, and finished up in Brescia at the Italian Institute for Advanced Culinary and Pastry Arts, with a couple of externships at internationally renowned restaurants thrown in between for good measure.''

"Cripes, no wonder you make a good cup of coffee and the best cornmeal muffins in the western hemisphere!"

"Mmm-hmm." Amusement danced in her eyes.

"You really enjoyed making a damn fool of me, didn't you?"

She burst out laughing, a ripple of sound as sweet as the music of the stream running down beside his house, and he was stunned by the transformation. He'd thought her eyes were her best feature, but he saw now that she had a lovely, sexy mouth, a beautiful smile. "I did get a kick out it, yes."

"I can see I'm going to have my hands full with you." Too bad his gaze happened to settle on her equally lovely breasts when he said that. Too bad, as well, that he couldn't control the inappropriate stirring in his loins.

She was a client, and that put her firmly off-limits as far as anything personal went. But it was a pity. She had the kind of subtle appeal that crept up on a guy. Under different circumstances, they could have enjoyed quite a fling together.

"Have I spilled something on my shirt?" she asked him, so pointedly that he realized he was still staring.

He cleared his throat and tore his gaze away. "No. I was just…thinking."

Suspicious as a Sunday schoolteacher patrolling the choir stalls in search of unseemly goings-on, she said, "About what?"

"The best place to start," he said, knitting his brows in what he hoped passed for a reflective scowl. "When we get to Vancouver, I mean."

"I should think, by then, you'll have had enough for one day."

He checked his watch and pushed away from the lunch

counter. "Could be. We're going to hit the Tacoma-Seattle area right in the worst of the rush hour, and who knows how long we'll be held up at the border crossing. Drink up, and let's get a move on."

They covered the stretch between Salem and Portland in chitchat which, though casual enough on the surface, in fact resulted in a whole slew of personal information being exchanged. That was the problem with the enforced intimacy brought about by spending hours on end in a car with someone. It made strangers seem familiar, and lowered a guy's guard to the point where he revealed things better kept to himself.

The conversation finally petered out though when she lowered her seat to a reclining position and, settling her sunglasses more firmly on her nose, let out a mighty yawn. *Cripes, if I was boring you, all you had to do was say so!* he felt like telling her.

On the other hand, her snooze did present him with the chance to make better time. Whistling under his breath, he kept one eye on her and the other on the road. When, after a good five minutes, she hadn't moved a muscle, he turned on his radar detector and let the speedometer needle inch up another notch.

"I'm watching you," she said, her disembodied voice floating up accusingly. "Slow down."

"I thought you were sleeping."

"Uh-uh. Just thinking."

"About?"

"You."

"Oh, yeah?" Her admission sent a strange jolt of awareness through his gut. "How so?"

"You're very handy in the kitchen. That steak you served last night was top-notch."

"So?"

"So did you do all the cooking when you were married, or is it a skill you picked up after the divorce?"

"Mostly after the divorce," he said, wondering why she

kept harking back to the topic of his failed marriage. "It was a question of doing that, or living on leftover pizza and beer."

"You could have hired a housekeeper."

"Not a chance," he said. "I don't need some woman underfoot all day, ironing my undershorts and overcooking the vegetables."

"That's a pretty sexist attitude! Not all housekeepers are women, any more than all good chefs are men."

"Somehow, I don't see myself living with a man, even one in a servant capacity. Alone and doing for myself suits me just fine."

"Do you ever think about remarrying?"

"I already told you, I'm lousy marriage material. But just in case you're wondering about my sexual preferences, I do like women. I just don't want one moving in on me."

"Well, I didn't think those were your bath crystals," she said, hinting pretty broadly that she'd like to know who did own them.

No dice, cookie! he thought. "But they *were* my condoms."

That shut her up. She pulled her glasses back over her eyes and didn't say another word for the next thirty miles.

Traffic started to build just north of Olympia, becoming so congested as it approached Tacoma that, rather than fight it, he swung off the I-5 onto Highway 16 and followed it west as far as Gig Harbor.

"There's got to be someplace decent where we can get dinner," he said, cruising down the main street, "and I need to stretch my legs."

"I offered to drive so you could take a break."

"Thanks, but no thanks! A nervous Nellie like you doesn't belong behind the wheel of a car like this. You've been hitting a nonexistent brake so hard this last hour, it's a wonder your leg hasn't fallen off."

"Because you drive like a maniac!"

"You forget," he said, pulling into a parking space half a block from a waterfront restaurant, "I spent a lot of years in a patrol car, chasing the bad guys."

"Well, you're not in a patrol car now!"

He stroked his hand down her face. "Relax, darlin'. We'll have a nice leisurely dinner, take a walk along the harbor, and by the time we hit the road again, the commuters will have gone home and it'll be smooth sailing all the way to the Canadian border."

She blinked slowly, giving him a close-up view of those ridiculous lashes, and nestled her cheek against his palm. "Promise?"

"Promise. Now let's eat."

They secured a table at the window and ordered wild salmon, caught that morning. It arrived flanked by asparagus spears, baby potatoes drizzled with butter and chopped parsley, and slivers of roasted red and yellow peppers.

"I guess that once we get to Vancouver," he remarked, as they finished off the meal with strawberry cheesecake and coffee, "the first thing I have to do after I drop you off at your place, is find a hotel. Any place close by that you'd recommend?"

"No. You'll stay with us."

"Us?" He finished his iced tea and got to his feet.

"With my mother and me."

"You're still living at home?"

"Temporarily. Until the baby's found."

"And then?"

She licked a smudge of strawberry syrup from her lip, once again drawing his unwilling attention to a mouth he was finding increasingly fascinating. "I'm not sure I'll stay in Vancouver."

"You think you might go back to Europe?"

"Possibly."

Why did he care? he wondered, ticked off by the stab of dismay he felt at the thought of her living half a world away. He'd known her barely twenty-four hours, for Pete's sake—just long enough to know she wasn't his type. Not really.

"To do what?"

"Work, of course." She toyed with the last bite of cheesecake on her plate. "My dream is to open my own restaurant one day, but it's no easy business to break into. More aspiring restaurateurs wind up broke or bankrupt within the first year of operation than just about any other enterprise. So, the more experience I bring to the job, the better my chances of succeeding."

"Won't leave you much time for marriage and all that stuff."

"Oh, I'll manage—when the right man comes along." She finished off the cheesecake and smiled mischievously. "Who knows? I might get lucky and find someone who shares my ambition, and we'll open a restaurant together."

"You want children, as well?"

Her eyes darkened with sudden grief. "I thought I did—until Angela was stolen. Now, I'm not so sure. If my baby were to disappear..."

He reached across the table and trapped her fingers. "Don't let the actions of one madman take away your dreams, cookie. Men like Thayer are the exception, not the rule."

"I hope so."

He liked the feel of her hand lying trustingly in his. He liked it too much. *Don't play with fire, Sullivan! Someone's going to get burned.*

"Time to move," he said, abruptly breaking the contact. "If I sit here much longer, I'll fall asleep. I'll settle up what we owe and—"

She reached into her purse. "Let me pay."

"Don't give me an argument, Linda," he said, unaccountably out of sorts suddenly. "I'll send you a bill when I'm done with the case. Meanwhile, go powder your nose, or something. And don't take long."

* * *

They crossed into Canada just after ten that night. By then, she could see the exhaustion in the slump of his shoulders.

"In view of the time," he said, following her directions through the city and over the Lion's Gate Bridge to the North Shore and West Vancouver, "maybe I'll take you up on the offer of a room, just for tonight—as long as your mother won't mind."

"She won't. In fact, she's expecting you." She pointed ahead, to the quiet lane curving left from Marine Drive. "Turn here. Our house is at the end, facing the water."

"What do you mean, *she's expecting me?*"

"I phoned her from the restaurant in Gig Harbor. See the white garage doors just beyond the lamppost? Pull in next to them."

"You're kind of sneaky, you know, going behind my back like that," he said. "It makes me wonder how far I can trust you."

But she heard the smile in his voice and knew he didn't mind that she'd outfoxed him this one time. In fact, he sounded relieved, and small wonder. He'd been driving for nearly ten hours, not counting stops, most of it on the free-way and too much of it in heavy traffic.

"Every bit as much as I trust you," she said, leading the way along the path to the house. "We're in this together, remember? Watch your step. The lighting's not too good along here."

Her mother met them at the front door. As she made the introductions, Linda saw, for the first time since Angela had disappeared, a tiny flicker of hope amid the anxiety in her mom's eyes.

"We're very grateful to you, for coming all this way to help us," she said, shaking his hand. "Linda tells me you're the best at finding lost children."

"Linda is too kind," he replied, slipping her the evil-eye behind her mother's back.

There were sandwiches and tea waiting, and a fire in the living room to ward off the chill of the onshore breeze.

"We want to do whatever we can to help, Mr. Sullivan," her mother said, pouring a cup and passing it to him.

He smiled, and touched her shoulder with a kindness Linda hadn't suspected in him. "You can begin by calling me Mac. Mrs. Carr."

"Only if you'll call me Jessie," she said. "I'm so glad Linda found you. With you in charge, I feel very hopeful that I'll soon have my family together again."

"You do know it might take some time and that I can't—?"

"I have a feeling it won't. I think you'll be more than a match for Mr. Thayer. I think he'll be sorry he ever tangled with you."

There was no missing the strain in his smile. "Optimism is good, Jessie, but please save a little strength in case…we run into any snags. It doesn't do to be overconfident."

She wasn't having any of that, though. "If Linda thinks highly enough of you to bring you here, I know my faith won't be misplaced. But I can see I'm making you uncomfortable, so I won't belabor the point further. Tell me instead about the book you're writing. Is it going to be a bestseller?"

They chatted idly for another half hour, but although Mac was charming and attentive to her mother's questions, Linda sensed the tension in him and was glad when Jessie announced, "With you on the job, Mac, I do believe I'll get a decent night's sleep for a change, so if you'll both excuse me, I'll leave you to unwind from the journey and take myself off to bed. Linda, I've put Mac in June's room, since it's not being used right now. The bed in there's a lot more comfortable than the pull-out sofa in the study."

"Thank you, ma'am. You're very kind," he said, standing up and folding the hand she held out to him in both of his. "Sleep well, and we'll talk in the morning."

"Thank *you,* my dear. Your being here makes all the difference."

The air fairly crackled with brittle tension in the wake of

her departure. "Well," Linda said, her nerves stretched taut as a wire, "we might as well call it a day, as well. Get your bag and I'll show you to your room."

But when she went to get up from the sofa, his fingers snapped around her wrist so unforgivingly she wondered her bones didn't crumble, and forced her back down again. "Not so fast," he said, with soft but unmistakable malevolence. "We're not quite done in here yet."

"We're not? I thought you were tired."

"Not nearly as tired as I'm ticked off."

"I don't know why!"

"Sure you do, cookie," he said. "So we're going to have a little chat in which I do all the talking and you do nothing but listen. I'm going to lay down a set of rules simple enough that even you can understand them. And if you choose to disregard them *for any reason at all,* then I'm out of here and you're on your own. Am I making myself clear?"

CHAPTER FIVE

"CLEAR? Hardly!" she said. "My mother's opened her home to you. She's expressed her appreciation for your help. I fail to see why that should have brought about your sudden change in mood. What's the matter—wasn't she grateful enough?"

As if clamping her to him in that iron-hard grip wasn't insult enough, he had the temerity to shake her, though less with the intent to hurt than to shock, she had to admit. "Gratitude is fine, when it's called for, but so far I've done little to earn it. What I don't handle well is being set up by someone I expect to be up-front with me."

"And you think I haven't been?"

"We both know you haven't, not when you let me walk in here unprepared for what I'd find."

"What you found, Mac, is a person who's been given reason to hope again. A person who'll face tomorrow with a little more encouragement than she was able to face to-day."

"I found a woman without a husband...one whom you've led to believe can expect a miracle. She seems to think I'm Superman."

"But that's not what's really bothering you, is it, Mac?" she said. "It's the fact that she's in a wheelchair. Well, shame on you! I thought you were a bigger man than to let a little thing like that throw you for a loop."

"A little thing?" He released her and wiped his hand down his face. "Maybe for you, Linda, but from where I'm sitting, it smacks of emotional blackmail. Your mother's in hell. It's written all over her face. Yet every time she looked at me, I saw the faith in her eyes, the absolute conviction

66

that I'm going to put an end to her misery—a conviction, I might add, which you put there, even though I've told you repeatedly that I can't offer any guarantees that I'm going to find that baby or bring her home alive.''

"Then tell her you're not sure you can live up to her expectations. Prepare her for the worst.''

"Oh, sure!'' he sneered. "As if she's not coping with enough already.''

"You're the one allowing a wheelchair to blackmail you, not she.''

"Damned right I am! And if that makes me less of a man in your eyes, learn to live with it.''

She regarded him soberly a moment. "If I'd told you ahead of time that my mother's disabled, would you have turned down the job?''

"I'd have been prepared to handle it better. I don't like surprises. I particularly don't like it when my so-called accomplice is the one responsible for them. One of the first things you learn in police academy is that if you want to live to see another day, you'd better be able to count on your partner, and I'm not sure I can count on you for a damn thing.''

"Meeting my mother was hardly a life-or-death situation.''

"I agree. On the other hand, you seem to get a charge out of keeping me guessing, and while it's amusing once or twice, I don't want you thinking you can make a habit of it. Showing me up for the fool I undoubtedly was in shooting off my ignorant mouth about your incompetence in the kitchen is one thing, but this business tonight was quite another. So here's the way things are going to pan out from here on: there'll be no more games. It's not a question of one-upmanship, or you against me. Either we're in this together, or we're not.''

"We are,'' she assured him, dismayed. "I'm sorry if you felt I blindsided you tonight. It did occur to me to tell you about Mom right at the start, but if you were going to help us, I wanted you to do so free and clear of any sense of guilt or obligation.''

''That no doubt explains why you parked your sweet behind on my doorstep and begged so pitifully to be let in,'' he said, but the ruthless cast of his mouth relaxed into a smile which took the sting out of his words. ''Talk about pulling out all the stops!''

''I was desperate, and you can surely see why, now that you know the situation here. This whole business with June and Kirk has been a nightmare pretty much from the day they met. Obviously my mom is limited in what she can do to help. My sister now needs psychiatric care—and please note I'm warning you ahead of time what to expect in that department—which leaves me the only one able to take affirmative action. And I couldn't do it alone.''

''I understand that. And I willingly agreed to come on board. But there'd better not be any more withholding information, or trying to do an end run around me. No sneaking behind my back, or leaving me wide-open to situations I'm not expecting. We've got enough uncertainty on our hands. Kirk Thayer's an unknown quantity and we have no idea how this is all going to play out. But one thing is certain: any man who steals a baby is unhinged. In my opinion, that's more than enough to contend with.''

''I understand,'' she said again, chastened.

''I hope you do. Because either you're completely upfront with me from now on, or the whole deal's off. It's your call.''

''There'll be no more withholding anything, I promise. I need you too much to risk having you walk off the job.''

''And I need some sleep.'' He raked his hand through his hair, and looked at her, his eyes troubled. ''Are you sure having me here isn't too much for your mother?''

''Quite sure. And don't ask that question in her hearing or she'll pin your ears back so far they'll meet behind your head!''

"Okay, if you say so." He nodded at the tea tray. "What about clearing up all this?"

"I'll take care of it, as soon as I've shown you to your room."

"We'll take care it *before* you show me to my room."

"I'm not the one who's been driving all day."

"But you are the one who's arguing with me—and right after I'd made it clear who's calling the shots around here."

She shrugged, gathered the cups, saucers and plates onto the tray, and stood back. "Fine. Pick that up and follow me."

In the kitchen, a small brass lamp with a parchment shade threw a circle of mellow light over the telephone nook. Smooth indigo flooring echoed the blue of the Delft tiles above the counters. Through the open window, night-scented stocks in her mother's flower garden filled the room with delicate fragrance.

"This is nice," he said, looking around. "Very nice. There's a real feeling of home here."

"Yes. We've known some very happy times in this house."

He leaned against the counter and watched as she covered the remaining sandwiches with plastic wrap, stored them in the refrigerator, and loaded the china in the dishwasher. Then, as she went to lock the back door and turn off the lights, he said, "You haven't said much about your father, Linda, beyond the fact that he left when you were a teenager."

"That's because there's nothing about him worth mentioning."

"How come?"

A silence descended, leaving a void filled by a host of unwilling memories, of the man who'd taught her to ride a bike, who'd read bedtime stories to her and June, who'd dressed up as Santa Claus and danced around this very kitchen with her mother in his arms. And who'd walked out on all of them when his pretty, vivacious wife became an invalid confined to a wheelchair.

"Because," she said coldly, hating the pain which, even all this time later, brought the sting of tears to her eyes, and hating Mac for being the one to revive it, "he hasn't been a factor in our lives for years."

"So he doesn't know about the baby?"

"No. And he wouldn't care, if he did."

She heard him move. Felt his unswerving gaze seeing into her mind as surely as she felt his breath on the back of her neck. "I know what it's like to grow up without a father, Linda. It isn't easy, and it isn't fair. Kids should have both parents, all the time."

"Yes, but there's a difference, you see," she said, her voice thick with feeling. "The pain of having a father die has to be just a little bit compensated for by the knowledge that he didn't have any choice in the matter. That if it had been up to him, he wouldn't have left. But when a father *chooses* to go—can't wait to get away, in fact—it doesn't leave a whole lot of room for doubt about how much he *didn't* care for his family."

"Why haven't you told me all this before now?"

"For the same reason that I didn't bleat about my mom having no legs," she said bluntly. "I'll pay for your help, but I'm not interested in buying your pity."

"How about simply accepting my help and my sympathy?"

"I don't need your sympathy. Save it for my mother who's already lost more than anyone should have to forfeit, and who stands to lose even more if she never sets eyes on her first grandchild again. And don't even bother accusing me of keeping secrets again, because my father has no bearing on any part of the problem my mother and sister and I are facing."

"Come on, cookie." He touched her lightly, caressing her nape. A nothing touch, just like his kiss that morning.

"This time, I'm offering a shoulder to cry on, not criticism or reprimands. Let me play hero at least once today."

"I don't need your shoulder. I'm not crying."

But she was. She always did, whenever she opened that particular door from her childhood, and remembered her mother's face, the day her husband left her alone to bring up a girl in her early teens, and another barely out of babyhood.

Mac didn't say a word to contradict her. He simply closed the remaining distance behind her and ran his hands over her shoulders and down her upper arms, the pressure warm and firm and comforting, which was a huge mistake on his part because it started the tears flowing in earnest.

"Don't be kind to me," she said, covering her face and trying to stifle the gasps shuddering through her. "I can deal with anything but that. Tell me I'm a fool, an unfeeling wretch, but please don't—"

"Shut up, Linda." The murmured command ruffled the hair on the crown of her head. Winding his arms around her waist, he cupped her elbows and drew her back until she stood cocooned in the shelter of his body. His chest pillowed her spine; his thighs cradled her hips. "Just shut up and lean on me. That's what I'm here for."

He touched her deeply with his gentleness, and with his kindness. They left an indelible mark on her heart which she knew would remain long after he'd left her life. It was a warm, fine feeling, and it occurred to her that she could have remained like that indefinitely, with him holding her secure against all the fear and darkness which made up both past and present.

Nothing stayed the same forever, though. Sometimes, love turned to hate; concern to indifference.

And once in a very rare while, something unexpectedly beautiful sprang from ordinary beginnings. She didn't know exactly when the tenor of his embrace changed, or how passion could encroach with such stealth that she was caught in its captivating web without being aware that she'd been trapped.

But she did know when his mouth slid down her neck and came to settle with searching, shattering effect just below her ear. And she knew, too, with stunning certainty, that unlike that morning's, this one could not, by any stretch of the imagination, be dismissed as a "nothing kiss."

This possessed the slow-building heat of a volcano, stirring the hidden layers of her soul, of her body, to simmering awareness. It came charged with implicit demands—for permission, for reciprocation. It stole without mercy, and left her helpless and quivering beneath its assault.

It left her wanting and shameless. Starving for the feel of a man's body pressed to hers in blatant hunger. She could no more contain her low moan of pleasure when his hands moved from her elbows to her breasts, than she could control the urge to reach behind and slide her palms with bold deliberation over the firm contours of his buttocks.

She turned her head. He found her lips. Found them parted, willing, hungry. She felt him, strong and hard and rhythmically insistent, against her lower back. And the kitchen, whose tranquillity moments before had been disturbed by nothing more earthshaking than the hum of the refrigerator, became filled with the sound of desire; of a man and a woman caught in the staccato hiss of breathless avarice. Of two bodies intent upon only one conclusion.

His hands roamed over her, traveling at random from her breasts to her hips, and further. To her thighs, to the subtle hint of cleavage between them. Fleeting touches only. Promises, not quite kept, of greater pleasures hers for the asking and his for the giving.

But they were in her mother's kitchen, and that sweet, beloved parent lay in her bed just down the hall, confident that she'd invited a gentleman to stay as her guest. Sure that at least one of her daughters knew better than to fall prey to the allure of sex without any guarantee of the emotional commitment that turned it from dross to gold. And if Linda was not cognizant of that fact, Mac was.

"I can't do this," he groaned, prying her away. "Not here. Not in your mother's house."

"Then where?" she asked, the question ragged with unspent passion.

He stepped away from her. Raised his hands high, beyond the range of temptation. Because he *was* still tempted. She saw the evidence he could not hide. It was printed on his face, stitched into his painful breathing—and sculpted *there,* beneath the trim fit of his blue jeans. She could have drawn the still-urgent length of him with her fingertip, so clearly was he revealed.

"Yeah," he said hoarsely, trapping her gaze. "That's right, cookie. Your eyes aren't deceiving you."

Unashamed at being caught staring, she touched her lips, wondering that they hadn't blistered from the heat of his kiss. "If this had happened last night, at your house, would you have stopped?"

"Probably not."

She sighed, all manner of lovely pictures floating through her mind. "Then I wish—"

"Don't push your luck," he warned her. "And don't go asking for trouble. You've got enough of that already."

Would he be trouble?

Oh, yes!

Could she handle it—him?

No. Not in this lifetime! He lived on a different plane, a whole world removed from her realm of experience. She should be thanking him for his restraint, not regretting it.

So why was she bleeding inside, as if something vital and indescribably precious had been cut away from her heart? Why did she feel as if, on top of everything else she stood to lose, she'd just been robbed of the most wondrous thing of all?

He was watching her, those cool blue-gray eyes tracking her every expression and reading it all too clearly. "Don't say it, Linda. Just go to bed and get some rest. You're worn-out and not thinking straight. You'll feel differently in the morning.''

Funny how kindness could soothe in one context, and slash in another. Not ten minutes before, she'd soaked up his compassion. Now it crushed her.

Willing her face and voice not to betray the pain she felt, she said, "I should show you where your room is, first."

"I'll find it," he said. "There can't be too many to choose from. The house isn't that big."

"It's the middle door on the right, down the hall on the other side of the front door. I'll leave a lamp on for you."

"Fine."

"Good night, then. Sleep well."

"Thanks," he said. "You, too."

As if!

Smothering the reply, she turned and walked away with as much dignity as she could muster, given that her pride trailed behind her, torn to shreds.

"I know he had money," Jessie said, of Kirk Thayer. "Far more, really, than his job seemed to warrant. He drove a very expensive car and was always showering June with gifts."

They were at the table in the nook off the kitchen, with the remains of breakfast still littering the table. The sun streamed in the window behind Linda's chair, making it difficult for him to read her expression. Her mother sat across from her, and he'd been assigned to the head of the table, the place where the delinquent husband and father should have been.

"Did he ever mention his family—parents, siblings, cousins? Anything that might give us a clue as to where he might be holed up with the baby?"

"Only that he had relatives in Portland. He wasn't very forthcoming about himself at all, probably because he knew I didn't approve of his live-in relationship with June."

"Why not, Jessie?"

"He was too possessive. He wanted her all to himself. That's what finally made her leave him. If he'd had his way, she'd never have set foot in this house again."

"And June never confided in you?"

"No. By the time the relationship ended, when she was seven months along, all she thought about was the baby. Kirk Thayer was the last thing she wanted to talk about, and I didn't like to press her. Perhaps I should have insisted more, but..."

"You couldn't have known what would transpire," he said. "Don't blame yourself for any of this."

"It seems to me that you're quizzing the wrong person," Linda chimed in.

It was her first contribution to the discussion, and he knew the reason she sounded so chilly had nothing to do with the fact that he was questioning her mother, and everything to do with what had taken place the night before.

"I agree," he said, flicking a glance her way before redirecting his attention to Jessie. "Is June up to answering a few questions, do you think?"

Again, Linda put in her two bits' worth. "She has to be. Otherwise we've wasted our time coming back here."

"Not necessarily," he said mildly. "I intend speaking to the people Thayer worked with, as well. But given that they lived together for several months, June's probably our best source for any personal history he might have divulged."

"Mom?" She turned to her mother. "Do we have to run this by her doctors, first?"

"I'm sure not," Jessie said. "As long as we keep them informed, just so they can be ready for any adverse reaction, I don't think there'll be a problem." She swung her chair away from the table. "We can leave as soon as you're ready, Mac."

"Let me give you a hand cleaning up in here first."

"We don't need your help," Linda informed him sourly. "Marjorie will be here soon."

"Marjorie?"

"My daily help," Jessie supplied, and winked at him before she left the room, as though to say, *Pay no attention to Linda. She's not a morning person.*

"Is it something I didn't say that you think I should have?" he asked, collaring Linda before she also took off.

She regarded him with lofty disdain. "I haven't the foggiest notion what you're talking about."

"Sure you have, cookie," he said. "You're in a snit about last night, and unless you want your mother asking awkward questions, I suggest you get over yourself."

He should have known better than to tangle with a woman trying to cope with her own sexual appetites, especially when they'd announced themselves so blatantly and gone unsatisfied. "Get over *your*self!" she spat. "My only feeling about last night is relief that we put an end to an ill-conceived idea before it got out of hand."

Ill-conceived? An unfortunate choice of words, he thought, but one which might have been all too appropriate had he not come to his senses when he did. "Glad to hear you say that," he replied. "Now prove you mean it and paste a smile on your face. June's depressed enough as it is, from all accounts. She doesn't need your long-suffering, poor-me attitude making her feel any lower."

"Allow me to know what my sister can and can't handle," she shot back, "and confine yourself to doing the job I hired you to do."

He folded his arms and fixed her in the kind of telling stare which, in the old days, could reduce hitherto smart and uncooperative suspects to babbling idiots willing to spill the truth at any cost. "Don't make me regret that decision, Linda," he said softly.

She bit her lip and glanced at her feet, clearly fighting the little demon inside urging her to tell him to take a running jump off a short pier. "I'm sorry. I'm a little…on edge."

"Understandably. Just remember I'm not the enemy here."

*   *   *

At first sight, June seemed better. She was dressed and sitting in the day lounge, instead of lying in bed in her room. Her hair was freshly shampooed, and she wore a little blusher to relieve the pallor of her cheeks. But on closer inspection, Linda saw the same emptiness in her eyes; felt the same lack of response when she hugged her.

"We've brought you a visitor, sweetie," she said, hiding her disappointment behind a too-bright smile. "This is Mac and he's going to find your baby for you."

A flicker of something—hope? despair?—crossed June's face. "Come along, darling," her mother urged, reaching for her hand. "Let's go find a quiet corner on the sunporch where we won't be disturbed."

She went willingly enough, a stick-thin figure moving like a sleepwalker being led back to the safety of the bedroom.

"Jeez," Mac said in a low voice, following behind with Linda. "How long has she been like this?"

"Nearly a month."

"She's in bad shape, cookie. Ready to snap at the slightest provocation."

"Yes." She swallowed the sudden lump in her throat. "You see now why I came to you for help?"

"Yes," he said, and caught her hand briefly, reassuringly. "I'll give it my best shot."

His best, she soon discovered, exceeded anything she'd expected. With skill and sensitivity he drew her sister out of the protective fog in which she'd hidden herself.

Within a very short time, he learned that Kirk Thayer had acquaintances but not many friends. That he seldom spoke about his ex-wife, but kept numerous photos of his son around the apartment. He was generous but used his wealth to control people. When he learned June was pregnant, he became obsessively concerned about her and the baby's health to the point that he forbade her to drive her car or leave the apartment without telling him where she was going and when she'd be back. He phoned her constantly from work, and insisted on accompanying her to every doctor's appointment. Although he became very upset when she told him she wouldn't marry him, he never showed any violence toward her or gave any hint that he'd resort to such extreme measures after the baby's birth.

"What can you tell me about his family?" Mac asked, shifting to another aspect of the man's history.

"Which one?" June asked.

For a moment, he seemed floored by her question. "Not his ex-wife and son, honey. I mean his parents."

"I know," she said. "But which ones?"

"Most people only have two."

"Not Kirk. He had his birth parents and those who adopted him."

"I didn't know he was adopted," Linda exclaimed. "You never mentioned that before, June."

"You never asked," she said.

"But why didn't you tell us anyway?" her mother said.

"Because you didn't like him, Mom. You didn't want to know anything about him."

"But I do," Mac said, gently drawing her attention back to the real issue. "Why don't you tell me everything he told you?"

"His mother—he always called her his *real* mother—gave him up when he was seven."

"Was he an only child?"

"No. He had a baby sister, but the mother kept her."

"Do you know why?"

"They were very poor. She could only afford one child."

"So he was placed for adoption and found a home with another couple?"

"Yes. And I think they were good people and treated him well. But he always wanted the Thayers, his real family. He spent thousands of dollars trying to trace his sister."

"Did he ever find her?"

"Yes. She lives in Portland."

Mac flicked a telling glance at Linda, his message clear. The Portland police had been contacted and found no trace of Kirk having been there in at least a year. Another dead end.

"You say his real family were called Thayer. Did he never take his adoptive parents' name?"

"At first. But he said he changed back to his birth name a few years ago—right after his marriage broke down, I think."

"Before you met him, then." Mac tapped his pencil against the notebook on the table next to him. "Do you recall his ever mentioning his adoptive parents by name? Was he in contact with them at all?"

"Not very often," she said. "But I thought they seemed awfully nice. They sent him gifts at Christmas and on his birthday. And when they found out I was pregnant, they sent me lovely baby clothes." Her expression, which had become quite animated, darkened, and she plucked at the skirt of her dress. "I still have them, but they'll be too small for her now."

"Never mind, darling." Her mother stroked her arm lovingly. "When Angela comes home, we'll buy her new things."

"She isn't coming home," June said, on a soft wail. "He's taken her away where we can't find her."

"It's my fault," her mother whispered, the courage that had brought her this far crumbling in the face of June's distress. "If I'd made him feel more welcome..."

"It's nobody's fault but his," Linda said staunchly, her heart breaking for her sister, and for the pain and guilt she saw in her mother's eyes. "And we will find her. Mac will find her." She glared at him. "Tell her you will!"

When he didn't immediately answer, June burst into tears.

"Tell her, damn you!"

He snapped his notebook closed. "Take your mother for a walk, Linda," he said calmly, giving away nothing of what he had in mind. "Leave me alone with your sister."

"Not a chance! Look at the shape she's—"

"Do as I tell you." His words, though softly uttered, nevertheless cut through her protest sharp as a whip.

"We'll be in the cafeteria," her mother said.

"We'll be right outside the door," Linda contradicted. "Close enough to hear every word. You'd better not upset her any more than you already have."

"Whatever." He dismissed her with a shrug and turned back to June. "Hey," he said, almost crooning to her. "Dry those tears, sweet thing. We're so close to cracking this investigation wide-open, I can practically taste success. Just a couple more questions, and we'll be there."

"I want my baby," she sobbed.

"I want that, too, June. So, tell me…"

"Come away, darling," her mother said, tugging at Linda's skirt. "You trusted Mac enough to bring him here. Now let him get on with the job."

He found them in the cafeteria fifteen minutes later, and strolled to their table, looking so carefully noncommittal that she knew at once he'd learned something significant which he wasn't about to share. However, he wasn't Detective Lieutenant Mac Sullivan on official business anymore. He was her paid employee—or would be, once he handed her a bill. And that gave her the right to know exactly what he knew, exactly as soon as he knew it.

"Well?" She eyed him balefully. "Kindly don't keep us waiting. How's June doing now, and have you found out anything useful?"

"To answer your first question, June was smiling when I left her, and in a much more upbeat frame of mind," he said, positioning himself behind Jessie's wheelchair. "As for your second, I've discovered a very serious loose end which should have been tied up weeks, if not months, ago. And if you haven't yet figured out what that is, Linda, you're not nearly as bright as I thought you were.''

CHAPTER SIX

HE WAS lying. Or if not that, then editing what he said. She'd have challenged him on it, if he hadn't bared his teeth in a smile on a par with a shark about to swallow her whole, and under cover of retrieving his notebook, which he conveniently dropped at her feet, whispered in her ear, "Button up, cookie! We'll get into this later when we're alone."

"Loose end?" Containing herself with difficulty, Linda struggled to remain civil. "Do you mind being more specific? In my opinion, this entire case is full of loose ends."

"I'm talking about paperwork—in this instance, official documentation naming June as the primary custodial parent."

Startled, she exchanged a look with her mother. "Do we have such a thing?"

"No, you don't," he said, answering before Jessie could open her mouth. "I asked June specifically if she ever applied to the courts, and she didn't. We need to rectify that. At once. Which means making phone calls, speaking with a family court expert, and possibly arranging for someone to act as power of attorney on June's behalf—that someone being you, Jessie."

"Drop me off at home and I'll get right on it," she said.

He planted a kiss on her cheek. "You're my kind of woman, sweetheart! I knew I could count on you to get the ball rolling."

"What can I do?" Linda asked, absurdly resentful that he was so free with his compliments toward everyone but her.

"You can direct me to where Thayer worked and help me interview his former colleagues. With any luck, by tonight we should have a more complete picture of the man, and be better armed to put a halt to his actions.''

"Let's meet at the house for dinner at seven," her mother suggested, with something approaching her former zest. "We'll have a round-table conference and pool our information, then see where to go from there.''

Whatever his other faults, Linda admitted to herself, Mac was turning out to be a real morale booster—at least as far as her mother and sister were concerned. Too bad she couldn't make the same claim for herself.

"I don't know why you're making such a fuss about this custody business," she said, after they'd driven her mother home in her specially equipped van and were headed across the bridge in his car, to the downtown office tower where Kirk had worked. "It strikes me as being a bit like closing the stable door after the horse has bolted.''

"That's because you don't understand how these things work," he said, giving her knee a patronizing pat.

If she'd had a meat cleaver handy, she swore she'd have chopped off his hand! "Why don't you educate me, then?''

"Well, it goes something like this," he said, weaving through the heavy midmorning traffic with what struck her as cavalier disregard for life or limb. "With no outstanding court order favoring June, police involvement, both here and in the U.S. or anywhere else for that matter, is limited to the point that it becomes virtually ineffective.''

"How were we to know that? And who expects to have to apply for custody of a child within hours of her birth?''

"Anyone with reason to think his or her right to that child might be in jeopardy, and why no one brought that to your attention before now stuns me. Without the proper documents, no police department has the authority to seize a child, unless there's compelling evidence either that the child has been unlawfully taken, or is in danger—danger, in this case, meaning that the abductor has a history of violence. Neither situation exists, and any attorney worth his salt could have told you that weeks ago.''

Loath though she was to admit it, Linda felt obliged to say, "I'm not sure June consulted a lawyer when the baby was stolen. I don't think she saw the need. She thought it was a police matter."

"Understandable, given the circumstances, but also unfortunate."

"Are you saying it's impossible to remedy the situation?"

He mulled over the question as she directed him to the underground parking area of Kirk's office building. "Not impossible, but here's the problem," he said, maneuvering the Jaguar with impressive confidence into a spot she'd have thought was scarcely wide enough to accommodate a motorcycle. "The courts are notoriously slow-moving. You, on the other hand, have retained me to locate your niece as quickly as possible—preferably yesterday! Should I uphold my end of the bargain and find Angela, what then do you expect me to do?"

"Return her to her mother, of course!"

"How?"

She stared at him, floored by such a patently unnecessary question. "By seizing her, and bringing her back here with all due speed. I'm surprised you even have to ask!"

"I can't seize her. And unless she's living in a state of squalor and neglect, I can't remove her from her present situation. And if you stop to think about what I've already explained about the way these matters work, you ought to be able to figure out why my hands are tied."

Her heart sank like a stone. "You don't have legal authority to remove her from her father's care."

"Exactly. But that's not the worst of it, cookie."

"It can get worse?" A fresh wave of dismay washed over her.

"It very well could, if Thayer has exercised the foresight to apply for his own custodial order. That would mean that if we tried to take Angela against his wishes, he could have you and me both arrested for kidnapping. If convicted, we'd be spending a lot of time in adjoining cells.''

She scrunched her eyes shut. "Oh, God! Does June know this?''

"No," he said gently. "I could see no purpose in telling her just yet, or your mother, either, and I'm sorry to be laying it all on you like this. Hopefully I'm throwing up obstacles that don't exist. But it seems only fair to warn you of the possible difficulties we might run into.''

"You did the right thing in telling me." She squared her shoulders. "It's better to be prepared.''

"I'm not suggesting we give up, you know.''

"I'm not, either. I'm not letting a creep like Kirk Thayer get the better of me.''

He grazed his knuckles down her cheek. "That's my girl! Now let's go talk to some people and see how much dirt we can dig up on him.''

There turned out to be very little.

"Kirk was competent, something of a loner, one of a hundred or more employees, and eminently forgettable. No one missed him when he was gone and probably wouldn't have remembered his name if it hadn't been splashed all over the front page of the newspapers in the days after he took off.'' Discouraged despite her earlier resolution not to let Kirk get the upper hand, Linda leaned against the wall of the elevator as it carried them back to the parking level from the vice president's glass-walled office on the twenty-eighth floor. "Got any more bright ideas, Detective Lieutenant Sullivan?''

"I think I should feed you. It might improve your outlook.''

"I'm not hungry.''

"Tough," he said, as the elevator doors hissed open. "I am. The only choice you have is where we go to eat.''

"I don't care.''

"Don't sulk, Linda," he chided, towing her unceremoniously behind him and bundling her into the car. "It's unbecoming in a woman your age. And don't take your frustration out on me. I'm not the enemy here, as I believe I've mentioned before."

"No, Kirk Thayer is—and he always seems to be one step ahead of us. Every time we think we're getting somewhere, we end up walking into a brick wall."

"But we're not beaten yet." He rolled the car toward the exit gate. "I'd even go so far as to say we've hardly started. I've still got a couple of tricks up my sleeve."

"Such as?"

He gave a Mr. Mona Lisa smile. "All in good time, cookie! Let's eat first. There must be a restaurant in that park we passed through, after we crossed the bridge."

"Several, as it happens."

"Choose one, then," he said, "and hang the expense. Lunch is on me."

"We could try The Teahouse."

"Fine. You're the navigator. Show me the way."

They sat at an outdoor table on the terrace, and ate grilled tiger prawns and scallops, accompanied by baby green salad drizzled with raspberry vinaigrette and washed down by chardonnay.

The weather was glorious; obscenely so, she thought, given the dark cloud hanging over her family. Sailboats danced on the waters of English Bay. The North Shore mountains lazed beneath a sultry summer sky. A breeze, light as a baby's breath and warm as a kiss, teased her face.

"Tell me what else you found out from June," she said, embarrassed by her guilty pleasure in the moment. "I know there was more than you let on about in front of my mother, and I've got a right to know what it is."

"I don't dispute that for a minute."

"So…?" She glared at him, wishing he'd take off those blasted sunglasses, which flung back twin reflections of the striped umbrella at the next table, but revealed nothing of what he might be thinking.

"So give your food a chance to digest before you start fulminating again."

"I don't have the time."

"Unless you want to burn out before we're halfway through this case, I suggest you make the time." He slid his glasses halfway down his nose and surveyed her critically. "You're looking a bit ragged around the edges. A couple of hours relaxing over a meal isn't going to make or break your niece's situation, but it'll go a long way toward relieving the pressure building up inside you. Enjoy the respite while it lasts, Linda, and save your energy for when you really need it."

Recognizing that to ignore the voice of wisdom and experience when she heard it was nothing short of foolhardy, she tried to follow his advice and found it not impossible. Of course, it didn't hurt any that she was with the most attractive man in town. Nobody looking at him—and plenty of women did—would have guessed he was a former police detective.

He looked supremely sophisticated and relaxed in his well-cut tan slacks and short-sleeved white shirt. Devastatingly mysterious behind his dark glasses. Elegantly trim and fit, as revealed by his breadth of shoulder and the tanned muscularity of his forearms. Even she had difficulty picturing him with a gun in his hand, prepared to maim or kill if need be. Yet she knew that lethal capability was as deeply ingrained in him as his deceptively lazy smile and casual posture.

"But there *is* more, isn't there?" she persisted.

"There's more," he admitted, but made her wait until they'd finished eating and were sipping iced coffee before he set down his glass and said, "Okay, what do you want to hear first: the good news, or the not-so-good?"

Apprehension foamed up in her at that. "The not-so-good. Get it over with, please!"

"Your father's back in town. He's been in touch with June."

"What?"

"You heard me. Martin Carr is back. Seems he somehow got wind of everything that's happened—probably through the newspapers or TV reports—and blew back into town to lend moral support."

"He wouldn't know moral support if it jumped up and bit him in the face!"

"Take a deep breath, cookie," Mac counseled drily. "You're fulminating again."

She struggled to contain herself, not because he said she should, but because Martin Carr had created enough upheaval in her life and she'd see him in hell before she let him go on another destructive rampage.

"That's better," Mac said, inching her water glass closer, and waited until she'd taken a calming sip before continuing, "Isn't it possible he's trying to do the decent thing for once?"

"No. He doesn't have a decent bone in his body!"

"What makes you so sure, Linda? Is it because he walked out on his family, or because he walked out on a woman in a wheelchair?"

"Take your pick," she said bitterly. "They both fit."

"Do you blame him for your mother's accident?"

"He was the one driving the car that put her where she is today, for God's sake!"

Clearly taken aback, he said, "I didn't know that. You haven't mentioned how she came to be injured, and I was hardly going to ask."

"I'll tell you anyway. My father is very charming, very handsome, and very suave. His philosophy has always been *Live life to the fullest,* a principle he interprets to mean doing what he pleases with whomever he pleases, regardless of the damage it might inflict on those he professes to care about. My mother adored him. All three of us adored him. We thought the sun rose and set on him. But..."

She stopped and fumbled in her purse for a tissue, afraid not that she'd cry, but that if she did, Mac would think her tears sprang from grief when they were inspired by anger.

Watching her with ruinous sympathy, he said, "The problem was that what he had at home wasn't enough."

She blinked, and managed to turn a choking sob into a caustic laugh. "What are you, a mind reader?"

He shook his head. "I know the type. For some men, one woman is never enough."

"So my mother found out, to her lasting cost and utter devastation."

He toyed with his coffee glass a moment, then said, "I venture to suggest that she appears to have got over the devastation. All things considered, she strikes me as a very well-adjusted woman."

"You weren't there. You didn't see how he hurt her, or how much she changed as a result of what he did. She used to be full of light and…and *movement*, and so in love with him it dazzled people, just watching them together. June was only a baby at the time, so she doesn't have much memory of the way they were, but I used to think they were more glamorous than movie stars."

"He must have played the role of romantic hero very convincingly."

"He did. He could turn the most ordinary day into something magical. He'd come home and, for no reason at all, waltz her around the kitchen when she was making dinner, or out onto the patio in a thunderstorm. He'd bring her roses every Thursday, because that was the day they met, and leave exquisite gifts on her pillow when he had to go out of town on business because he so much hated being away from her." She swallowed, and looked out to the far horizon where the Gulf Islands floated in the heat haze. "And then…"

"Then she discovered that he didn't go alone."

"Yes."

"Someone told her?"

"She overheard two of her friends talking in the ladies' room at a Christmas dinner-dance. One of their husbands had seen him checking into a hotel in Montreal, with a woman hanging all over him. It was someone my mother knew, someone she'd welcomed into her home, and who was actually sitting at their table that night."

"And?"

"Mom confronted him. He didn't deny anything, she walked out, he went after her, insisted on driving her home, it was snowing, he drove off the road and plowed into a tree. You've seen my mother. You know how the story ended."

"I'm sorry."

"Not half as sorry as he'll be, if he dares show his face at our house!" She let out a trembling sigh and looked him squarely in the face again. "I think I'd like to hear your good news about now."

"June gave me the name and address of Thayer's adoptive parents." He reached for her hand and pulled her to her feet. "Next stop, San Francisco, cookie, so let's go make flight reservations. With any luck, we'll be there by tomorrow night at the latest."

"Why don't we just phone them to find out what they know?"

"This isn't an official investigation, Linda. They don't *have* to cooperate, and it's a whole lot easier for them to hang up on us than it is to ignore us when we're standing with my big foot jammed inside their front door. Not only that, it's easier to get a fix on people when you're talking face to face with them. Often it's less *what* people say than *how* they say it, that counts. A trained eye can usually spot evasions and tension that might not be apparent just from the spoken word." He slid behind the wheel of the Jaguar. "So where's the nearest travel agent?"

"In Park Royal shopping mall." She pointed to a fork

in the road as he pulled out of the parking area in front of the restaurant. "Turn left here and follow the signs to the bridge."

The mall came loaded with everything a person could possibly need or want, including gourmet foods, art, custom jewelry, and enough boutiques selling overpriced clothing to keep the couturier business in clover for a decade.

They left there with plane tickets, pâté de foie gras, imported cheese, Cornish game hens, wine and flowers, and took the scenic lower road to Jessie's house.

"She's got company," Linda said, as he pulled up next to a black BMW. "Either that, or the daily help's won the lottery."

But Mac wasn't fooled. The old radar clicked in the minute they walked in the house and heard the sound of voices coming from the patio in the back garden, and he knew what they'd find. "Linda," he said, dumping their purchases on the kitchen counter and trying to forestall her before she got to the French doors. "Honey, wait!"

He was too late. By the time he reached her, the well-dressed man sitting at the wrought-iron table opposite Jessie had risen to his feet. And Linda had turned rigid with shock.

"Hello, baby," Martin Carr said.

She ignored him. Looked clean through him, and said to Jessie, "What's he doing here? Why have you let this man into our house, Mother?"

"Honey," Mac said again, laying a restraining hand on her shoulder. "Take it easy, okay?"

She shrugged him off. *"Mother?"*

"Your mom and I are merely talking, baby," Martin Carr explained, running a nervous hand over his mane of silver hair. "In times of trouble, families have to pull together."

"Pull together?" she said with biting scorn. "What would you know about something like that? The only thing you've ever shown any talent for is pulling things apart, then bailing out when you get caught."

A pained expression crossed the still-handsome face. "You have to let go of the past, baby. It doesn't do any good to hang on to—"

"Don't you have somewhere else you ought to be? Some popsie's boudoir, perhaps? Or have you lost your touch? Could it be that the ladies don't fall at your feet any longer, now that you're past your prime?"

Carr flinched and Mac, watching the exchange, decided if she'd looked at him the way she looked at her father, he'd probably have been impotent for a week. "We haven't met," he said, stepping between her and her father in an effort to fend off full-scale war. "I'm Mac Sullivan."

His handshake was firm, his voice gravelly with emotion. "Jessie told me about you. We're deeply grateful to have you on board. And my little girl's lucky to have a man like you at her side." Ignoring Linda's snort of revulsion, he gestured to the bottle in a cooler on the table. "Won't you join us in a glass of wine and bring us up to speed on what you've found out."

"You're not privy to what we've found out," Linda spat. "It's none of your business."

"Linda," her mother interjected quietly, "whether or not you like it, Martin is your father, and he is here at my invitation. I'd ask you please to treat him with the same courtesy you'd show to any other guest in our home."

"You don't seem the least bit surprised or disturbed to see him, Mom," she retaliated. "Is it because you've known all along that he's been visiting June, and just forgot to mention it to me?"

"Your mother didn't know anything," Martin said, laying a hand on the back of Jessie's chair. "She had no idea I was back in town until this afternoon and she doesn't deserve your contempt. If you're angry with anyone, baby, it's with me, not her."

"I am not your baby," she whispered, spitting out each word from between clenched teeth. "And as far as I'm concerned, you're not my father."

Carr backed off, the dapper, well-preserved image of a

man in his late fifties who'd done his best to pass for forty, suddenly aging right before everyone's eyes. He coughed, and smoothed the silk cravat at his throat with an unsteady hand. But if he was shocked at being disowned by his first-born, Jessie was shattered.

"For pity's sake, Linda, take that back!" she gasped, tears welling in her eyes.

But Linda was having none of it. "I sorry, Mom, but I can't. I won't. You might choose to forget what this man has done to our family, but I never will."

She pivoted on her heel and stalked back inside the house, leaving the three of them not knowing quite where to look or what to say. A moment later, the front door slammed, echoing through the house like a rifle shot.

Jessie let out a cry of distress and turned her gaze on Carr in unspoken appeal. "Go after our daughter, will you, Mac?" he said, bending to put his arm around her. "I'd go myself, if I thought it would do any good, but I think I can do more by staying here with my wife."

"Sure," he said.

He found her at the end of the lane, sitting on a slab of flat rock overlooking the water. "Make room for me," he said, hunkering down next to her.

She shuffled over without a word and continued staring out to sea. He gave her another ten minutes or so to get herself together, then said, "We might as well talk about what happened back there, cookie. You said some pretty harsh things."

"I told the truth," she said, her voice as remote as her expression. "I hate him."

He debated how to answer and decided truth deserved truth, however unpalatable it might be. "Maybe you do, but your mother doesn't. She's still in love with him."

He might as well have shoved her face-first off the rock and into the sea. She rounded on him, spluttering with out-rage. "You're crazy!"

"Uh-uh!" He shook his head. "She looks at him the way

my mother used to look at my dad. And for all his faults and shortcomings, I'd go so far as to say your father's not entirely indifferent to Jessie.''

Her glare shifted from outrage to horror. ''I think I'm going to be sick!''

''You'd do better to accept something you can't change. You've seen your mother's heart broken once. Are you willing to let it happen again—and know that this time, you're the cause?''

''I'll speak to her. Remind her how happy we've been without him. When it comes down to making a choice between him and us, she'll choose us.''

''She shouldn't have to choose at all.'' He sighed and pulled her to lean against him. ''You're not a kid anymore, Linda, and neither is June. You know nobody's perfect, that people make mistakes. Give the old man the chance to prove he's learned from his.''

''You can afford to be charitable toward him. You're not the one he betrayed.''

''No, I'm not. But he's no fool, cookie. He knows he screwed up big time, as a father and as a husband. Isn't it just possible that he's trying to make up for past mistakes by being here now, when your family's in trouble?''

''We'll get through this without him, the way we got through all the other tough times. I don't need him, and neither does my mother.''

''You're wrong,'' he said. ''He's exactly what she needs.''

She turned on him, spitting like a wild cat. ''Who are you to tell me what she needs? You don't even know her, and you certainly don't know him!''

''Being a quick study of character is essential in detective work. I have great faith in your mother's instincts. She lost the use of her legs, Linda, not her brain. She managed without you all the time you were away in Europe. She doesn't need you as her watchdog now.''

"So what am I supposed to do? Just roll over and play dead?"

"No, darlin'," he said, hugging her closer. "That wouldn't be any fun at all. What you do is go back to the house, announce you're making dinner and invite him to stay."

"I'll poison him!"

He laughed and kissed her hair. "Then I'll cook dinner, and you can sit with him and your mom, and make small talk."

"I'd rather have my teeth pulled!"

"You'll do it," he said in her ear. "You'll do it because Jessie needs someone to lean on right now, and you and I are taking off first thing tomorrow. You'll do it because June needs all the moral support she can get while you're gone."

She stared at the sun sliding down behind the mountains on the big island offshore. And as late summer dusk stole over the place where they sat, the resistance and anger seeped out of her. She buried her face against his neck and he felt her tears hot on his skin. "I really loved him once, you know," she sobbed.

"He's loved you all along, cookie. How could he help himself?"

"He's got a strange way of showing it."

"It's a guy-thing," he said. "We don't always know the right things to do or say."

One thing he did know, though. Holding her like that felt absolutely right. And when she lifted her head, nudging her lips with his felt right, too.

She needed to be kissed, he reasoned. To make her feel better. If it made him feel pretty damn good, too, it was because he enjoyed playing Boy Scout once in a while.

She had a delicious mouth. Warm and sweet and generous. She held nothing back. She fit in his arms as if she'd been designed exactly for that purpose. When he deepened the kiss, she responded. There was none of the awkward bumping of noses or any of that other clumsy stuff to tarnish the moment. It all felt absolutely right.

The slab of rock, still warm from the day's sun, lay shielded from the lane by a screen of low-growing bushes. He'd made love in less private places, including the back seat of a patrol car on one regrettable occasion. He felt her faint trembling; knew she'd be ready for him, that they could do it quickly, and he could make it special enough that she felt desired. Special enough to wipe out the shock and anger of meeting her father again, and leave her glowing with a sense of well-being.

"Let's go home, cookie," he said, putting her from him before lust overcame decency. She didn't need the complication of sex with her employee. And he didn't need the responsibility of trying to fill the empty space in her heart left by her father when he took off all those years ago.

It wasn't right, after all.

CHAPTER SEVEN

DINNER was a tense affair although, to give her credit, Linda did a spectacular job of the meal, throwing together a feast in record time.

At Jessie's insistence, they ate in the formal dining room, with candles and sterling and all the good stuff usually brought out to honor guests, though Mac had little doubt that, had it been just the three of them as originally planned, they'd probably have made do with a more casual setting at the round table in the breakfast nook.

"Isn't this pleasant?" Jessie said, glowing with delight as Martin wheeled her to one end of the long mahogany table. "Mac, I want you here, on my right and you, Martin...well, you sit in your old place opposite me, of course."

Linda didn't say a word about that. She didn't have to. The frosty sheen in her eyes spoke volumes, none of them fit to be aired aloud. Instead, "Will you pour the wine, Mac?" she asked, pointedly snubbing Martin, even though he'd have been the logical choice for the job, since the ornately carved cellaret holding two bottles of sparkling burgundy stood right beside him. "And pass this along, if you don't mind."

"This" was a serving of chilled watercress soup intended for her father. Mac supposed it was to her credit that she didn't wing it over the polished surface of the table with enough speed to slop it into the poor guy's lap.

"Smile," he murmured, giving her neat little tush a pinch as he passed behind her with the wine bottle.

She let out a tiny squeak, turned bright pink and plopped

down on her chair. Taking his place opposite, he eyed her over his soup and said blandly, "Delicious!"

Despite herself, she smiled, the tension lessened fractionally, and they made it through the first course without open war being declared. When it was done, he scooped up the empty dishes and followed her as she marched into the kitchen with the soup tureen.

"See?" he said. "That wasn't so bad, now was it?"

"It was revolting, and I'm stomaching the whole ridiculous charade for my mother's sake only. If I had my way, that man would be out of this house so fast, his head would spin."

"Well, don't take your frustration out on the salad," he said, backing off to a safe distance as she swirled hazelnut oil and tarragon in a jar, flung the concoction into a bowl of curly endive and proceeded to toss it about with the vigor of a matador tormenting a bull.

She speared a morsel on the end of a fork and stuffed it in his mouth. "Spare me your advice and taste this instead. Does it need more seasoning?"

"No," he said, doing as he was told. "The smell coming from the oven, by the way, is out of this world. You must really know your stuff, if you can turn plain old guinea hens into something this special."

"I ought to. I spent enough time and money learning how. And trying to soften me up with sweet talk isn't going to work, so save your breath." She cast an eye over the fig and orange-ginger sauce simmering on the stove, and tucked the wooden salad bowl in the crook of her arm. "Round two coming up," she said, and tromped out of the kitchen with him bringing up the rear.

It was unfortunate that they approached the dining room just in time to hear Martin say, "You're as beautiful as ever, Jessie."

Linda let out a furious "*Aargh!* Did you hear that?", did an immediate about-turn, and came up smack against Mac's chest.

"What the devil...!" He caught the salad bowl as it flew out of her hands—just! A second later, and he'd have been wearing its contents. "Yes, I heard. He paid your mom a compliment. Would you be happier if he insulted her?"

"I'd be happier if she'd just show him the door. Talk about being handed a line!"

"What if he's telling the truth for once?"

She fixed him in a withering stare. "Don't tell me *you're* buying into his weasely ways, as well!"

"At the risk of being branded equally weasely," he said, hardly able to keep his face straight, "I think you need to take stock of what's really going on here, cookie. Your mom went to a lot of trouble with her appearance tonight, and I doubt she did it to impress you or me—or does she always dress for dinner?"

She pursed her mouth into a fetching pout, reminding him of how silky it had felt when he kissed her. No doubt about it: she grew on a guy, big time!

"No," she mumbled, clearly hating to have to concede the point. "Only when she has guests—which is all he is or ever will be. So if he's laboring under any other impression, he's going to be very disappointed because I will not stand idly by and see him break my mother's heart a second time."

Mac set the salad bowl on the edge of the hall table and taking her by the shoulders, turned her around so that she could peep through the crack of the open door. "Linda," he said in a low voice, "take a good look at your mom's face and tell me honestly what you see."

"She's happy," she whispered forlornly. "That's what worries me. She hasn't glowed like this in years."

"Look past the obvious and see what's behind the smile. Your mother's a strong, mature woman, Linda. She doesn't need you acting as her baby-sitter or her bodyguard. She's survived a lot worse over the years than spending an evening being gracious to the father of her children."

"How can you be so blind?" she sputtered. "He's using

our troubles to win her sympathy and worm his way back into her affections!''

He stroked the nape of her neck soothingly and tried for a more positive spin on the situation. ''Or else your troubles have made him put someone else's needs ahead of his own, for once, and he genuinely wants to help.''

A grimace of annoyance crossed her face. ''I should have known better than to confide in you in the first place,'' she said, wriggling away from him and grabbing the salad bowl. ''You men always stick together.''

On that note, she flounced into the dining room and left him to pick a shred of endive off the front of his shirt before he followed. ''Well, that went well, Sullivan,'' he said wryly. ''I can hardly wait to see what you've got lined up for an encore!''

Her mother *had* taken extraordinary pains with her appearance, Linda had to admit. She'd changed into a cherry-red skirt and matching lace top and hung a small diamond pendant at her throat—the latter one of Martin Carr's gifts from a happier time.

Under a pretense of following the conversation swirling around her, Linda picked at her food, submerged in a misery she was at a loss to understand. She'd been sure she was past caring about anything her father might do or say, which made the pain his presence now caused her all the more distressing.

She didn't normally snipe at other people, or go out of her way to make them feel unwelcome. Yet despite her best intentions to remain aloof and civil, she'd found herself uttering nasty, barbed little comments aimed at keeping her father on the defensive, and might have peppered the entire meal with more of the same had conscience and her mother's stricken expression not shamed her into silence.

What bothered her the most, though, was that her father accepted her attack with a humility that filled her with equal amounts of guilt and anger.

Why didn't he retaliate? Lash out at her and thereby justify her condemnation? By what right had he acquired the ability to make her feel lower than a worm when he himself had earned that ignoble rank?

Her relief when dinner finally ended left her almost light-headed. Indeed, when she jumped up from her seat to clear away the remains of the meal, a momentary dizziness caught her by surprise, causing her to stagger slightly and clutch at the table for support.

"Linda?" Her mother regarded her anxiously. "Are you all right?"

"Perhaps you should sit down," her father said. "You look rather pale, bab—my dear."

But Mac, his gaze scouring her face, inquired malevolently, "Too much wine with dinner, cookie, or is it the vitriol you ingested with your food that's giving you the heebie-jeebies?"

She couldn't look him in the eye; couldn't bear the scorn she heard in his voice. Her father might have been willing to overlook her behavior, but Mac clearly wasn't.

"Neither," she muttered, shame riding over her face in heated waves. "I just got up too quickly, that's all. I'll be fine in a moment."

"You've overdone it today, that's the problem," her mother decided, "and no wonder, what with seeing June, and all the running around you did afterward, then making dinner on top of it. Take Mac out to the garden and enjoy what's left of the evening. Your father and I will finish cleaning up in here, then bring coffee out to the patio when we're done."

It was the best offer she'd had in hours, one she'd have accepted in a flash had Mac not outmaneuvered her. "Better yet, I'll give you a hand in here, Jessie, so that Martin and Linda can spend a bit of time sorting out their differences and hopefully arriving at some sort of truce."

She could have smacked him. Throttled him! How dare he interfere? "I really don't think—!"

"Then it's about time you did," he said sharply, making her ashamed all over again. "Particularly when it comes to other people's feelings."

Incensed, she glared at him. "What I was about to say, before I was so rudely interrupted, is that I'll be much better company after I take a shower. I didn't have time before dinner, but after cooking in this heat, I really feel ready for one now."

As improvisation went, it was pretty feeble, but she had to hand it to her father for being gallant enough to accept it at face value. He simply nodded and said quietly, "In that case, I'll lend a hand with the cleanup, too. It'll be done that much faster then."

It was illogical of her to feel excluded as the three of them trooped into the kitchen and left her to her own devices. Unreasonable that she wanted to know what they were talking about. And just plain silly to assume their laughter, which she could hear even after she locked herself in her bathroom, was directed at her.

"It's all my father's fault," she muttered, adjusting the spray in the shower and shampooing her hair with a vengeance. "And as for Mac Sullivan...well, he can keep his opinions and advice to himself, except as they pertain to finding Angela. I don't give a rip what he thinks about my attitude toward dear old dad."

But the plain fact was, she cared very much, about everything Mac thought and said. And that was the most ludicrous thing of all.

She'd known him only three days, for heaven's sake! Nobody should matter that much on such short acquaintance, especially not to a woman who'd prided herself throughout her adult life on keeping her head where men were concerned.

She had no business finding his kisses so captivating. As for her aching disappointment when he'd backed away from their passionate encounter that afternoon, well the sooner she brought an end to that kind of nonsense, the better! She knew what happened to women who fell under the spell of men like him. She'd seen it firsthand with her mother.

Curious to find out why the house seemed so uncommonly silent when she returned to her bedroom, she pulled on a silk caftan and stepped out of the French door, which opened directly onto the west side of the garden. Beyond the lawn, her mother was showing off to Martin Carr the roses she cultivated with such loving care every summer. They were talking, their heads bent close as he leaned over her wheelchair, but the low murmur of the ocean at the foot of the garden masked what they were saying.

The same was not true of the sounds floating out of June's room as the French door suddenly swung open, just a few yards away from where Linda stood.

"Sure," she heard Mac say. "I'm sorry, too, but I'll make it up to you as soon as I wind up this case...yeah, it's turning out to be a royal pain in the butt, but I can't very well back out now...I always am, darlin', you know that. You take care now, and I'll see you soon."

She heard the click of the phone being turned off, followed by the sound of him whistling under his breath and the rasp of a zipper opening. But over and above that, she heard the wrenching thud of her disappointed heart.

Until that moment, she'd conveniently forgotten that he had relationships beyond those he'd shared with her. Forgotten that he kept condoms in his nightstand—and why. There *were* other women in his life, and the realization spurred her to rash reaction.

Driven by a need to see him, to remind him of *her* place in his life, she went to his door, not sure what she expected to say or how he might respond to her presence.

Sensing her shadow at the threshold, he glanced up. "Hey! Feeling better after your shower?"

"Much," she replied, swallowing her panic at the sight of his suitcase lying open on the bed.

"Uh-huh." He continued to regard her expectantly. "Something I can do for you?"

"I heard voices in here and—"

"Yeah," he said. "I was on the phone."

"I see." *To whom? What's her name? What else do you call her, besides 'darlin'?* She cleared her throat. "It looks as if you're packing already."

He opened the closet and swept his clothing from the hangers. "That's because I am."

"Why so soon? Our flight doesn't leave until three o'clock tomorrow."

"I'm sleeping in the study tonight."

The quiver of uneasiness skating down her spine this time bore no relation to that which had prompted her to show up at his door in the first place. "May I ask why?"

"So that Martin can sleep in this room."

"What?"

"You heard, Linda," he said. "Your father's staying here, and you can hardly expect a man his age to make do on a pullout sofa when there's a perfectly good bed he can use instead."

"He has no right to be here at all!"

He shrugged with such weary disdain that she cringed. "Your mother doesn't agree. I'd even go so far as to say he might have wound up in her bed instead, if she weren't afraid it might shock you into an early grave."

"Are you telling me *she* asked him to stay?"

"You got it, cookie. At least for the entire time we're in San Francisco, and maybe indefinitely."

"I don't believe you!"

"That's your problem."

He went into the adjoining bathroom and piled his shaving gear, toothbrush and toothpaste into a black leather bag, the entire process accomplished with such brisk economy of movement that she felt compelled to remark, "You seem annoyed."

"You noticed? Bully for you."

"Are you angry with me?"

"Right again." His laugh jarred the tranquillity of the

evening. "But don't worry, I won't let it keep me awake tonight."

His indifference was worse than a slap in the face. Shaken, she said, "If it's because of the way I feel about Martin Carr, I can't help it, Mac."

"Sure you can. You just choose not to."

"You don't know what it's like to have your father walk out of your life without warning."

He stopped in the process of zipping his suitcase closed and pinned her in a searing glance. "Oh, but I do. And I know what I'd have given to have him walk back in again. *Anything,* Linda. And *everything.*"

"You weren't betrayed by your father, the way I was by mine."

"You think not? You think I wasn't angry that he put his job ahead of his family? That I didn't rage out loud at him for deserting us—for dying, so that some faceless stranger could live?"

"It's not the same. He didn't have any choice in the matter. My father did. He walked out on us."

"And lived to regret it."

She ground her teeth in disgust, all her earlier feelings of fondness, of desire for him, fading. "What's the use in discussing it? I can see he's completely won you over to his side."

"You need to get over this whole idea you cling to that people have to take sides, and recognize instead the advantage of remaining neutral until you're sure you have all the facts. But that's a pretty adult concept and you're so busy acting like a spoilt child that I don't expect you to grasp it."

"Don't patronize me, Mac," she snapped. "And don't presume to know more about my father than I do. His sudden concern for his family comes a bit too late in the day for me to place much faith in it."

"Gee, I'm sure glad you're not my ex-wife," he shot back. "I'd hate to be on the receiving end of such a punitive attitude. Not that you care what I think, I'm sure. Anyone so convinced she's right and the rest of the world is wrong is hardly likely to waste much time worrying about other people's opinions."

"Why are you making me out to be the villain here?" she cried, crushed by his unfeeling attitude.

"Why can't you cut the guy some slack and give him the chance to win back your trust? Your mother can—and she stands to lose a hell of a lot more than you, if she finds she's made a mistake."

"It's too risky."

"Life's full of risks." He shook his head and when he spoke again, his tone had softened. "You take a chance every time you cross the street, cookie. Every time you get behind the wheel of a car. Every time you use a bank machine and walk out with a wallet full of cash. You don't need me to point out there are a lot of desperate people in the world, and one of them could be watching, waiting to snatch your purse and knock you to the ground when you least expect it. Yet you do all those things anyway, without a second thought."

"This is different." Her voice faltered. "I'm afraid."

"You weren't afraid to confront me, even though you thought I was the next worst thing to the devil. You aren't afraid to go after Thayer."

"I would be, if I didn't have you to help me. I trust you, Mac."

"No, you don't. You just pay lip service to the idea. But at bottom, you don't really trust any man—maybe not any woman, either. If you did, you'd hear what I'm trying to tell you now. You'd give Martin the benefit of the doubt. And you'd respect your mother's belief that death is the only thing that stands in the way of repairing a relationship with enough good left in it to be worth the effort."

"All I hear you saying, though not in so many words, is that I'm wrong and everyone else is right. And maybe you're not as far off the mark as I'd like to think, because it certainly seems that I made a mistake about you."

"And why is that?" he sneered. "Because I dared to disagree with you?"

"No," she said, her voice breaking. "Because I thought you cared about me. You kissed me as if you did. You made me think you wanted me. But I can see now that none of it meant a thing to you. It was just a way of trying to coerce me into seeing things from your point of view."

"In other words, you *don't* trust me. Point proven. Case closed. Good night." He dismissed her with another shrug, hauled his bag off the bed, and headed down the hall to the study.

She hated him. She really did. He was arrogant, opinionated, and ill-informed. And still she wanted him! If he'd charged back into the room and swept her into his arms, she'd have gone willingly.

Chagrined to find herself on the brink of tears, and wanting only to hide in her own room until she'd regained some semblance of control, not just of the childish urge to cry, but also of the conflicting emotions he aroused in her, she spun around.

Her father stood framed in the open French door, blocking her escape. "You seem upset, Linda. Is there anything I can do?"

"You've done enough already," she said vehemently. "Everything was going smoothly until you showed up. Now it's all turned sour."

"Let me try to put it right again."

"And how do you propose to do that, Martin?" she asked, hardening her heart against the shadow of pain which filled his eyes at her use of his name.

"I just want to help. To lend my support."

"In case you haven't noticed, we've had to manage without your help or support for nearly fifteen years."

"I know." He lifted his shoulders helplessly. "Guilt's a funny thing, Linda. It can swallow up a man in so much shame that he can't face those he hurt. Worse, it drives him to punish himself by making the people he loves the most, despise him.''

"And your point is?"

"I'm trying to make amends. Your mother's prepared to give me another chance. Is there no way you can do the same, and let me help you through this terrible time?"

"I'm no longer a child. In case you've lost track, I'll be twenty-nine next April."

"That doesn't make you too old to need a father."

"Okay, then let me put it this way: I don't need *you* for a father."

He sighed and inspected his feet, his hands; the walls of the room, and the portrait hanging there, commissioned one Christmas, of her and June with their mother. A family of three women, and no man in sight. And finally, when there was nothing else left, he looked at her again, his face etched with sorrow. "What's it going to take for you to forgive me, Linda? To turn to me again?"

"There's nothing. You weren't there when I needed you. I learned to do without you a long time ago."

"And that's it? There's nothing else you'd like to say?"

"That's it."

"You don't want to tell me what a jerk I've been?"

"No, thanks."

"Then let me say it for you. I'm a loser. A fool. I screwed up the best thing that ever happened to me and I deserve all the scorn you can heap on my head. The world would be a better place without me in it. If I had a decent bone in my body, I'd go find a deep hole and bury my miserable self in it. I don't deserve a second chance and I forfeited any right I might once have had to care that my only grandchild is missing." He paused and looked at her again. "Have I missed anything?"

"That just about covers it," she said, furious to hear her voice cracking with tears.

He nodded and stepped aside, making space for her to

leave the room without having to touch him as she brushed by. "Good. Feel better?"

"Yes," she choked.

"Too bad I don't," her mother said, rolling her wheelchair out of the shadow of dusk and stopping next to him. "Linda, when you insult your father, you insult me, too. I loved him enough to bear his children, Angela is as much his grandchild as she is mine, and I welcome his offer of support at a time when we need to pull together as a family. I'm shocked and grieved that you can't recognize the courage it took for him to come here today, admit to his mistakes, and ask to be allowed to carry his share of our trouble. *Ours,* Linda—mine *and* yours."

Beleaguered on all sides, she said, "I don't understand how you can be so forgiving, Mom!"

"Perhaps because it's never occurred to you that there might be another side to the story, which you've never heard."

"Are you trying to tell me it was *your* fault he left us?"

"I'm telling you that it takes two to make a relationship work, and two to break it. No one but the parties involved ever really understands the dynamics that bring a man and a woman together. But I'll tell you this: if you ever fall in love—*really* in love—you'd better adopt a less rigid attitude than you're prepared to show to your father, because there's a lot of forgiving required to bring harmony to a marriage, and until you've been there and tried it, you're in no position to criticize how others go about achieving it."

She brushed her hands together and tapped her former husband's arm. "I think that just about covers it. Come along, Martin. I want to show you the pictures of the girls at their graduation. Linda looked a lot happier then than she does now, but hopefully that'll change, once she's had a chance to think about what I've said."

Mac decided against joining Jessie and Martin for a nightcap, as she'd suggested. They had a lot to talk about and sort out, and hardly needed him hanging around to witness it. So he stretched out on the sofa bed in the study, and watched TV for a while. Then, as darkness fell and the house sank into that quiet period prior to its inhabitants falling asleep, he turned on the lamp and helped himself to a paperback from the bookshelf covering one wall of the study.

But he found his attention wandering and eventually tossed the novel aside and faced up to what was really bothering him. *How the hell had he managed to become so embroiled in the lives of strangers? More to the point, how had he let a snippy little wench like Linda get under his skin?*

He knew better. Knew that, in giving in to his attraction to her, he compromised the objectivity he needed to bring the case to a successful conclusion. But against his better judgment and definitely against his inclinations, he found himself thinking about her and regretting that he'd spoken to her so harshly. Wondering if she was able to sleep, or if, like him, she was remembering how it had felt when he'd kissed her.

Restlessly he switched off the lamp and paced to the window. The garden lay in darkness but, a mile or two out to sea, a cruise ship ablaze with lights sailed by on its way to Alaska. In fact, when he leaned out of the window, he could hear the faint sound of music carrying over the water.

And much nearer, the equally faint sound of someone crying.

He scanned the patio, straining to see, and caught a glimpse of pale movement on the bench under the grapevine. He knew it wasn't Jessie. He'd heard the hum of her wheelchair as she passed by his door on the way to her bedroom, fifteen minutes earlier. And he hardly thought it was Martin.

A smart man, especially one who'd decided, less than thirty seconds before, that he'd do well to keep his distance from Linda Carr, would have crawled into bed, pulled the covers over his head, and refused to let that sad little whimper cause him to lose a moment's sleep. But then, a smart man would have thought twice before shooting his mouth off about the way she was handling her father's sudden reappearance on the scene.

You can't afford to take every cause and make it your own, the chief detective had cautioned him, when he'd first joined the plainclothes' division. *Your job is to uphold the law and apprehend the criminal. But that's not to say you shouldn't leave room for a little compassion every now and then.*

Pity he hadn't remembered that sooner. It might have spared her her present misery—and him the obligation to try to alleviate it. "Just keep things short and simple, Sullivan," he cautioned himself, swinging one leg over the low windowsill and dropping silently to the smooth flagstones outside. "Just stuff a tissue in her hand, tell her to dry up, and forget any ideas about lending her a shoulder to cry on."

But there was something else his chief had told him. *You're lousy at taking advice, Sullivan, and even worse at following orders. If there's no trouble brewing out there, I can always count on you to make some. Talk about being a beggar for punishment!*

And he forgot about that, too. Because she barely had time to recognize who it was looming over her in the dark before he lowered himself to the bench beside her, and took her in his arms.

CHAPTER EIGHT

HE'D booked them into executive class on the flight to San Francisco, and she was grateful. The wide console between their seats allowed for no nudging of elbows or knees; no intimate brushing of thigh against thigh, or shoulder against shoulder. Nothing which would betray the electrifying effect he had on her. If he wanted to touch her, he had to make a point of reaching across the distance separating them to do so.

Not that he showed any such inclination. Other passengers looking at them or listening to their conversation would have assumed they were merely colleagues planning strategy for an upcoming business conference—which, she supposed, hindsight showed wasn't so far off the mark as it might seem.

"I'm hoping to set up a meeting with the Wagners tomorrow," he said, settling comfortably into his seat as the Air Canada jet banked over the Gulf Islands and started its journey south. "I can't see doing it any sooner. We were over forty-five minutes late leaving Vancouver, which puts us close to the dinner hour by the time we land at SFO, pick up our car rental, drive into the city and check into our hotel."

"Oh," she said, trying to look and sound intelligent, which was no mean feat considering her thoughts were in total chaos. "I see what you mean."

Intelligent? She turned to the window and rolled her eyes in self-disparagement. *Stilted and stupid* was closer to the mark!

"At least we know they're in town and not planning to leave anytime soon."

She spun back to face him so abruptly that her neck gave a protesting crack. "We do? How?"

"I phoned their house from the hospital yesterday, after I'd spoken to June."

"But you said you didn't want to talk to them long-distance. You said—"

"I didn't mention *why* I was calling. I just wanted to establish they were in residence. No point in wasting time and money going down there if nobody's home, is there?"

"How did they sound? Do you think they'll cooperate with us?"

"I didn't actually speak to them in person. Jackson answered the call and announced rather grandly that sir and madam would be at home tomorrow if I had legitimate business with them and cared to make an appointment."

"Who's Jackson?"

"I guess he's the butler or manservant, or whatever you call people like him these days. Very British and proper. We might have a bit of trouble getting past him. He didn't sound the type to let just anyone in the front door. But Jessie gave me a copy of the baby's birth certificate, which names Thayer as the father, and that should prove we're not just a couple of slick salespeople trying to fleece a genteel old couple out of their life savings."

"It never even occurred to me that we'd need proof we're connected to Angela, but I should have known you'd think about it. You think of everything."

"It's part of my job to cover all the angles, Linda. That's what you're paying me for. And you've already got enough on your mind, without worrying about details like that." He surveyed her intently. "Although I must say, you seem to be holding up pretty well, all things considered."

"Do I?" She turned her face to the window and closed her eyes, shutting him out before he saw past her precarious facade of indifference. But how did a woman ignore a man who, less than twenty-four hours earlier, had taken her to the brink of total sexual surrender, who'd seemed to desire her as much as she desired him, but who, at the last minute, had suffered an attack of scruples which left them both in a state of disheveled frustration?

It hadn't started out like that. The way he'd come swooping down on her where she huddled on the patio had frightened her into letting out a little squeak of alarm. It had taken her a moment to realize whose arms had wrapped around her, and whose shoulder she was leaning against, and whose voice was whispering in her ear, "Ah, darlin', is it what I said earlier that's the cause of all this carrying-on?"

"Don't flatter yourself!" she'd sniffed, trying to push him away. "You're not important enough to warrant your own crying binge!"

It hadn't been a complete lie because she'd found herself overwhelmed by everything and everyone that day. And it had been better than wailing, *Nobody likes me! You're all lined up against me, and it's not fair when all I'm trying to do is put things right again!*—and thereby handing him reason to believe that while she might look like an adult on the outside, she was endowed with the mental age of a three-year-old.

"Then what?" he'd crooned, pinning her arms against his chest as she squirmed to get away. "Is it your father?"

Of course, her father! And her mother, too. Jessie's reproof and disappointment had hurt, no question about it. She and her mother had always been such a firmly united team, one she'd thought nothing could destroy.

Yet within hours of his coming on the scene again, Martin Carr had managed to swing popular opinion in his favor, and she'd been shocked at how easily he'd caused a rift between them. In her heart, though, she'd known the spat with her mother would pass. Nothing could really undermine a relationship founded on such a solid basis of trust and affection.

Nor had it. They'd made up first thing that morning.

Her relationship with Mac, however, rested on much shakier ground and was much harder to define. He should have been nothing but the expert she'd hired to find the baby, but in the space of only a few days, he'd assumed a more pivotal role. The single thread of their connection had split into several strands and woven together around a core of feelings for him which she could ill afford to indulge.

Angela was who mattered. *Hers* was the face which should be crowding her mind every time she closed her eyes. And yet, even knowing that within twenty-four hours, she might discover the baby's whereabouts, might soon hold her in her arms again, Linda's thoughts persisted in returning to last night.

He'd plunked himself down next to her and thrown one arm around her shoulder. "Stop fighting me," he'd ordered, his voice dark and velvety as the warm summer night. "Regardless of how royally we tick each other off on occasions, we're still a team."

"I suppose you call all your women *darlin'!*" she blurted on an overwrought hiccup, vividly conscious that he wore only a pair of dark briefs. "I heard you, after dinner, on the phone. *See you soon, darlin'.* You take care now. And that's not all. You said I was a pain in the butt, as well!"

"Yeah." Laughter laced his voice. "And ain't it the truth!"

He shouldn't have laughed at her. And she shouldn't have tried to smack him in the mouth for it. Feeling so fragile inside that she feared she might splinter into a thousand pieces did not justify violence.

Not that she'd succeeded in her intent. He was much too fast for her, catching her hand and pinning it behind her back with lightning speed. "Not nice, cookie," he'd drawled, something sleekly dangerous layering his voice and smothering the laughter. "And not very smart, either. You ought to know better than to take on a man trained in the lethal art of stopping an opponent—dead, if need be."

"Well, don't blame me! It's your fault."

"And how do you figure that?"

"You make me say and do crazy things. You belittle me to your other *darlins'!*"

Another wave of hilarity had overtaken him. She'd felt his chest heave with it, his breath shudder. And she could hardly blame him. She sounded completely deranged!

"I think my sixty-year-old mother would be very flattered to know she's still got what it takes to make a twenty-eight-year-old foam at the mouth with jealousy."

"I am not foaming!"

"No, of course you're not," he chortled. "You're fulminating. Again!"

His merriment had been contagious. Realizing how ridiculous she was being, she relaxed in his arms. A smile twitched her lips. A bubble of laughter rose in her throat, gurgled out of her mouth, and the next minute they'd both been choking as they tried to stifle their gales of mirth.

On a whim, she'd reached out, plucked a handful of grapes from the vine growing beside the bench and pelted him with the fruit. Some missed their mark; others he caught and hurled back at her with telling accuracy.

"You'll wake the neighbors," he warned, chasing her the length of the garden when she slipped away from him. "You'll get me arrested."

"Good!" she retorted on a whispered shriek, racing onto the beach with her nightdress billowing around her ankles. "It's no less than you deserve!"

He caught her almost at once, bringing her down on the sand in a flying tackle which almost knocked the wind out of her. But she wriggled away, heard the delicate fabric of her nightgown rip as she escaped, and didn't care. Just for a little while, all the stress and fear which had dogged her every move for too long floated away, and she felt carefree and...*joyful.*

She'd raced into the sea, taunting him. Thrown water in his face and dared him to follow, fully aware that he'd accept the challenge and make her pay for it.

He came after her and she retreated until the waves

lapped around her hips. She saw the gleam of his smile in the moonlight and knew retribution was at hand.

He flung himself forward in a flat dive, sending up such a wash of spray that she was soaked all over and her night-gown clung to her like a second skin. Then, just as swiftly, he disappeared beneath the surface. She felt his hands close around her ankles and her balance shooting out from under her. The next minute, she'd been gasping for air as the milk-warm waves closed over her head.

They'd wrestled, an uneven match to be sure, but playful nonetheless. Their bodies had clung, drifted apart, coiled around each other in a surreal kind of dance. She knotted her fingers in his hair. He imprisoned her hands behind her back. Loomed over her. Jeered at her futile efforts to escape him.

And then, without warning, the mood changed. The laughter died. Exuberance slid into desire. His hold shifted from roguish restraint to urgent invitation.

For a moment, he held her at arm's length, like a sea god hoisting a trophy aloft. Drops of water spiked his lashes, and rolled like a shower of diamonds over his shoulders. His hair gleamed blue-black in the moonlight. His chest heaved, matching the breathless rise and fall of hers.

His gaze slid over her, and came to rest on her mouth. "Gotcha!" he murmured, and pulled her close.

His kiss tasted of passion, hot and sweet as honey cara-melized over a slow-burning flame. Scorching. Torching.

She wound her arms around his neck and let the swell of the incoming tide lift her so that her legs floated up and around his waist. Her nightdress ballooned around her, a dim white cotton cloud caught in the languid ebb and flow of the sea. It hadn't mattered that she wore nothing under-neath.

His hands cushioned her, brought her snugly against him. She felt the urgent throb of his flesh nudging her belly. Felt the scalding rush of heat between her legs and knew that he discovered it, too, when he touched her there.

He groaned against her mouth, filling it with the sound of her name. Dragged his lips to her ear and whispered how he wanted to please her. Except he hadn't phrased it quite like that. Shocking and thrilling her at the same time, he'd said, "I want to feel you come," and stroked his finger over her flesh in graphic encouragement.

An arrow of sensation had darted through her, its path broadening as it burst free. She uttered a half sob, aching for completion and weak with desire. The hair coating his chest scraped lightly over her nipples, rousing them to an excruciating awareness, which spread to the farthest extremities of her body.

He touched her again, a more potent and insistent caress this time. "Yes?" he asked hoarsely.

"Yes!" she gasped.

He guided her hand to his groin, urging her to release him from the clinging fabric of his briefs. He was hard as steel, smooth as silk, as ready for her as she knew she was ready for him.

It had been at that crucial point that the Carrs's next door neighbor turned on his porch light and threw open his back door. "Go do your stuff, Tiberius," he commanded, shooing his golden lab outside.

The dog meandered through the garden, stopped awhile to sniff through the bushes edging the property, then emerged onto the beach where he immediately picked up Linda's familiar scent and, with a joyful yip, came galloping through the shallows toward her.

"Cripes!" Mac dropped her like a sack of potatoes.

"He's friendly," she'd spluttered, swallowing a mouthful of water.

"Easy for you to say," he muttered grimly, returning his most prized possession to the safety of his briefs.

Of course, the mood, the moment, were ruined. Embarrassment and dismay eclipsed magic and moonlight. He'd been gallant enough to turn so that she was shielded by his body as she struggled to cover herself with the clammy folds of her nightgown, but he'd shown no sign of regret that they'd been so rudely interrupted.

On the contrary, when she'd reprimanded Tiberius for straying onto the beach, Mac had expelled an uneven breath and said, "Don't get after the dog. He's got more brains than I have."

"Linda…?" His voice, overriding the monotonous whine of the jet engines, startled her out of her reverie.

She stared at him, confused. "I'm sorry. I was miles away. Did you want something?" *Like me, perhaps? Or are you thanking your lucky stars you didn't have to follow through with what we started last night?*

"I asked if you felt you'd made some sort of peace with your father."

She supposed that was as good a description as any. An awkward hug was probably about as much as either of them could hope for, given their long alienation. In fact, it was considerably more than she'd expected when she'd followed Martin to the beach that morning.

"I'd like to apologize," she'd said, catching up with him as he walked barefoot along the sand, "for the way I acted yesterday. I'm afraid I wasn't at my best and I'm sorry for what I said. It seems to mean a lot to my mother that you're here, and that ought to be reason enough for me to treat you with courtesy. You probably wish I could accept you as wholeheartedly as she's able to do, and the best I can do right now is tell you that I'll try, but it will take time. Just how much, depends on you."

He hadn't replied, nor had she anticipated that he would. But as she turned away, she happened to glance at him and saw the solitary tear tracking down his face.

She shouldn't have cared. Heaven knew, she'd wasted enough tears on him over the years. But the silent dignity of the man as he tried to control his quivering lower lip, and the suffering she suddenly saw so clearly in his eyes, touched her with humility.

Mac was right. People *did* make mistakes all the time,

some with the kind of far-reaching effects, which could change the course of lives, and she ought to know. In the clear light of morning, last night's escapade with him had shown itself for what it really had been: a serious lapse in judgment that might well have resulted in an unplanned pregnancy, and certainly had left her with a badly bruised heart. What right had she to castigate her father when she herself was as full of human error as the next person?

Afraid she might embarrass Martin if she let him see how moved she was, she began retracing her steps to the house. She'd gone only a few yards when he spoke.

"Thank you, baby," he said, so softly the words floated away on the morning breeze before she could hold on to them.

Electrified at how swiftly he'd taken her back to her childhood with those words, she'd half turned her head and nodded. It was the most she could manage. The lump in her throat had been too huge to allow for more.

They hadn't communicated directly again until it was time to leave for the airport, and he'd come to the door to see her off.

"I'm relying on you to look after my mother while I'm gone," she'd told him, as Mac loaded their luggage in the car.

"I won't let you down."

It had been on the tip of her tongue to tell him he'd better not, but she refrained. What was the point in taking one step forward, if it was followed by two steps back? So she'd hugged her mother and said, "I'll be in touch as soon as there's anything to report."

"We'll be waiting for your call, darling," Jessie said, hugging her back. "Good luck."

She turned to her father again, not sure what either of them expected of the other. This time, though, he'd been the one to take the initiative. "Be careful," he'd said, and caught her in a swift, hard hug, which took her breath away less for the energy behind it, than from the shock of feeling his arms around her. It had seemed so familiar. So right.

She'd bolted to the car, afraid once again that she'd betray her feelings in tears. Mac had eyed her speculatively but thankfully made no comment. The last she'd seen of her parents as the car backed away from the garage, they'd been side by side at the front door, their hands raised in farewell. A perfectly ordinary couple doing the perfectly ordinary thing as their daughter left home.

Except, of course, in their case, it wasn't ordinary at all. It was, she supposed, leaning back in her seat and staring at the perfect curve of blue sky beyond the aircraft window, nothing short of miraculous.

"You're not being very forthcoming today, cookie," Mac observed. "Getting you to talk is worse than pulling teeth."

She turned her head and looked at him. "I could say the same for you."

He shrugged. "I'm planning the best line of attack with the Wagners."

"How diligent of you, thinking about the job ahead," she said, ticked off at how easily he seemed able to dismiss the events of last night. Did he have to be so relentlessly down-to-earth all the time? Couldn't he have said *something* to let her know she hadn't been the only one swept away by the magic of the moment?

Her waspish tone did not go unnoticed. "How else do you suggest I pass the time between here and there?" he asked, all innocently raised eyebrows and sweet reason.

"Well, let's see. Like most men, you seem to think you're pretty hot stuff. Why not sip champagne and come on to the flight attendant?"

"It's too early in the day for champagne, and I outgrew putting the moves on flight attendants when I hit my late twenties."

"And how old are you now?" The question popped out,

unrehearsed, as she struggled to come to terms with her complex reaction to the man beside her.

"Thirty-seven. Old enough to be embarrassed at having compromised a woman's reputation by almost seducing her in public." He bent a disconcerting glance her way. "That *is* one of the things you've been stewing over, isn't it—the fact that, last night, I didn't pick up where we left off when the dog next door finally left the party?"

"Actually," she said, too annoyed with him for reading her mind so accurately to care about lying to his face, "I was wondering how old you were when you joined the police force."

"Twenty-two. Right after I graduated from university with the ink still wet on my criminology degree.... You tasted of toothpaste, you know. And smelled of shampoo and body lotion. I found it very attractive."

She didn't want to be attractive to him. She wanted to be alluringly, fatally irresistible. She wanted him to look at her with eyes heavy with desire; to take every opportunity that came his way to touch her, casually if others were watching, intimately if they were not.

"You needed a shave," she said.

"I needed to have my head read." He reached across and played loosely with her fingers. "If I'm going to make love to a woman, Linda, I don't want to be keeping an eye out in case the neighbor or the people in the next room walk in on us. It doesn't exactly enhance my performance."

If he made love, he said. Not *when*. What a sublimely courteous brush-off!

"It hardly matters to me, one way or the other," she replied huffily. "What happened last night took me by surprise, but I won't get taken in like that again."

"Nor I," he said. "Look, there's the Golden Gate Bridge. We'll be landing shortly. Better return your seat to the upright position and stow your hand luggage—"

"I know the drill, thank you very much."

But she didn't, not where he was concerned. He kept her

guessing too much. She had no idea what he was really thinking. Was it his police training which had taught him to hide his inner feelings so well, or was some woman—his wife, perhaps?—responsible?

They stayed at the Hyatt in Union Square, not in adjoining rooms nor even on the same floor. She'd barely finished unpacking before Mac phoned.

"I've got news," he said. "We'll talk over dinner. Meet me in the lobby in half an hour, and don't bother dressing up. We'll make it casual."

They found an Italian restaurant a few blocks away, a sprawling barn of a place where the chefs cooked steaks and fish over huge charcoal grills. Despite what he'd said, she bathed and changed into a pretty, narrow-fitting lime-green dress, added chunky gold earrings and bracelet and a straw bag with matching sandals.

"Okay, here's the scoop," he said, as soon as they'd ordered and the waiter had left them with a tray of antipasto and a jug of wine. "I spoke to Mrs. Wagner herself, and we're invited to join her and her husband for cocktails, tomorrow at six."

She was so surprised that she forgot to be annoyed that he hadn't complimented her on her appearance. "Cocktails! My goodness, how did you manage that?"

"I told her we were Angela's aunt and uncle, in town on vacation, and that we'd like to stop by and say hello."

"Uncle? *You?*"

"Well, why not? It's a role I'm familiar with, seeing that I've got more nieces and nephews than I can keep track of. And I didn't think we'd be quite as warmly received if I'd introduced myself as the retired police detective out to nail her adoptive son's hide to the wall."

"I guess not." She took a sip of wine. "So we're supposed to be brother and sister?"

"No. Just for tomorrow night, we're husband and wife."

"I'm not sure I want to be married to you," she said,

suppressing the surge of excitement that bolted through her blood at the mere thought of such an arrangement, "even if it is only for one evening."

"Well, look at this way, cookie. People tend to ask questions of strangers who show up out of the blue and claim they want to find a missing baby. I don't have a whole lot of background information about your family that I can just toss out as if it's part of my history, and that just might arouse their suspicions. But I can give a very convincing performance of new husband not quite sure of his facts, and turn to my pretty little wife for verification of things I'm unsure of."

"I suppose that makes sense."

"Of course it does," he said smugly, chewing on a fat green olive. "On top of which, older people tend to look fondly on newlyweds. Here's the thing, though: leave me to do most of the talking. We don't want to screw up what might well turn out to be the biggest break we're going to get in resolving this case."

"And I'm just a congenital idiot who can't string two words together without tripping over her tongue!"

He smiled and raised his glass in a toast. "You're a peach, darlin', did I forget to mention that? Just show your dimples, act suitably smitten with your husband and you'll do just fine. Oh, and we'd better dress up for the occasion. People who have a butler called Jackson probably don't wear blue jeans when they receive company. Did you bring something spiffy that'll do the job?"

"If I didn't," she said, smarting at the implication that she needed sprucing up, "I've got all day tomorrow to shop, and there's Nordstrom's and Neiman Marcus within walking distance of the hotel. The question surely is, do you have something classier than what you're wearing now?"

"I'll do my best not to embarrass you," he said, batting his long dopey eyelashes at her. "But in return, you've got to polish your manners. Taking pot shots at your doting new husband kind of spoils the impression we're trying to convey. You're going to have to smile, darlin', and look at me as if you worship the ground I walk on. Can you do that?''

All too easily, Linda thought glumly. *The problem will be remembering it's all just an act.* ''If you don't go out of your way to provoke me, then yes.''

''You're sure of that?''

''I'm sure.''

''In that case,'' he said, topping up their wineglasses, ''you won't mind if I run a little test by you, just to be on the safe side.''

''Test?'' She didn't like the way he was looking at her, like a fox about to enter the henhouse. ''What kind of test?''

''Nothing illegal,'' he said easily. ''Just your standard newlywed quiz. Let's begin with the basics. How did you and your husband meet, Mrs. Sullivan?''

''That's easy. I went to Oregon to find him—''

''You went to Oregon looking for a husband? How quaint!''

''No, of course that's not why I went! Stop putting words in my mouth.''

''So sorry,'' he said, sounding anything but. ''What was the reason, then? And please don't say you went looking for an ex-cop to help you find your abducted niece, unless you want to blow our cover completely.''

''Well…um…um…''

''Okay, let's skip that one and go to the next. How long have you known each other, dear?''

''Four days.''

''And you're married already? My, my, you give new meaning to the term 'anxious bride!'''

''Four months, then!''

''I see. And where did you meet?''

''…I don't know. In Canada?''

''I thought you'd spent the last two years in Europe?''

''Oh, all right, then! We met in Paris. Satisfied?''

"No need to get testy, dear. We're just interested in getting to know our granddaughter's Canadian family. Your husband's the youngest of four boys, isn't he?"

"No," she said, shooting him a self-satisfied smile. "He's the eldest of five."

"Really?" He beamed expansively. "Are they all charming and handsome like him?"

She choked into her wine. "Actually, he's the ugly duckling, but don't let him know I told you so."

"Did they all become police detectives, too?"

"No. He's the only one."

He slapped the flat of his hand on the table. "Okay, out of nine questions, you blew the answers to eight. I think it's safe to say you flunked the test with flying colors."

"I got three right! You *are* the eldest of five, you can't prove you're more charming and handsome than your brothers and you told me yourself that you're the only one who joined the police force."

"And letting that last little item of news slip out was the most disastrous of all your gaffes, dear lady. People, particularly strangers who might have something to hide, tend to become very closemouthed when they discover a detective in their midst, even if he is there in an unofficial capacity."

Discouraged, she slumped against the leather banquette. "I never thought of that. Maybe pretending we're married isn't such a good idea, after all."

"Sure it is. If you just stick to what you know and keep your mouth shut the rest of the time, we'll be just fine."

"Leave the lying to you, in other words."

"I prefer to call it embroidering the truth."

"This whole business is beginning to make me very nervous. What if the Wagners are hiding Thayer? What if they deliberately mislead us to throw us off the scent?"

"The only way to prevent that is to practice being Mr. and Mrs. Sullivan on vacation in San Francisco until we're letter-perfect. We can't afford to arouse their suspicions, or pose any kind of threat. If we do, we'll be out the door before the first drink's been poured.''

"Well, I wasn't planning on showing up with a gun tucked in my bra, if that's what's worrying you.''

"Not that kind of threat, cookie," he said with a laugh. "I'm talking about making them feel comfortable enough to let their guard down, which won't happen if they suspect we're not who we claim to be, or if they sense your hostility toward their son. That's why we need to polish our act, and since we have only tonight in which to do it, I suggest we get right on it.''

CHAPTER NINE

BY THE end of the meal, they'd exchanged enough life stories to fill a book, and worked out a fictional version of how they met, when and where they married, and where they now lived.

"I've told you things I've never revealed to another living soul," Linda confessed, as they strolled back to their hotel through the soft August night.

"Are you saying no one else knows you're afraid of heights and spiders? Holy cow, cookie, that gives me a real edge on keeping you in line!"

She was so immersed in thought that it took a moment for her to realize Mac had laced his fingers through hers and was swinging her hand back and forth, the way a man might with the woman he was dating. "It's not so much *what* I've told you," she said, loving his touch and how protected she felt when she was with him, "as it is the feeling that I've known you much longer than I actually have." She threw him an astonished glance. "I can't believe I told a man I met less than a week ago, about Arthur Hipwell."

"The high school creep who tried to get you in the sack, and when he didn't succeed, told the rest of the basketball team you were easy?" He curled his lip in contempt. "It's at times like that that having a big brother comes in handy."

"Or a father."

"Do you ever wonder if Martin's the reason you've never trusted a man enough to have a serious relationship?"

"I think it had more to do with not trusting myself, but I'm learning. Take our present situation, for instance. We're operating under false pretenses and might be walking into

128

trouble when we meet the Wagners tomorrow. Danger, even. Yet, I'm not afraid, because I feel safe with you."

He gripped her hand more tightly. "Hold on to that thought, cookie, especially if we hit any rough spots. Don't you be the one to rush to the rescue. Trust *me* to bail us out."

"I will," she said, refusing to give credence to the little voice inside whispering, *What if the reason you feel so safe with him isn't so much that he's the right man for the job as the fact that he's the right man for you?*

It was absurd to allow such thoughts to flourish. Almost as absurd as the letdown, which hit her like a fist to the solar plexus when, after clamping a possessive arm around her shoulders and standing so close to her in the elevator that she could feel his every breath, he left her outside her hotel room without so much as a kiss on the cheek.

She might have weathered the disappointment better if he hadn't lingered at the door, and traced his thumb along her jaw, and looked at her as if he had more on his mind than the brusque good-night he eventually offered. But hadn't that been his trademark from the minute they'd met—leading her to expect one thing, then doing another?

She was a fool, she decided savagely, kicking off her smart sandals and stepping out of the lime-green dress. And a beggar for punishment, too! How many times did he have to reject her at the last minute, before she got the message that, when it came right down to the wire, he didn't want her?

Mac took the stairs up the extra four flights to his floor, in the faint hope that the exercise would kill the urge to hammer on her door and finish what he'd started last night.

It wouldn't be smart, and it wouldn't be fair. He knew himself too well—and crazy though it sounded on the surface, he also knew her too well, even if she'd come into his life only days before. A man didn't achieve detective lieutenant status without becoming a pretty good judge of character, and she...

"Cripes, she's an open book!" he panted, letting himself into his room and leaning against the door. "Even a rookie could read her."

And even a rookie knew better than to mix business with pleasure. Instinct was all very fine, as long as it was backed up with cold, hard fact and logic.

"So consider the facts of this case, Detective," he admonished himself, pacing to the window and scowling on the late-night crowds in Union Square. "You and she don't fit. She's got city lights in her eyes, and ambition in her heart. Notions of opening a five-star restaurant, of making a name for herself. Do you see her being happy in Trillium Cove where the big news of the day is that the mail came in fifteen minutes early? Do you see yourself in a long-distance relationship? Moving to some metropolitan area where the only sound to disturb the night is the wail of sirens? Face it, buddy, that's one of things you were glad to leave behind when you quit the police force!"

Logic. Cold hard fact. One and one, which added up to two. Trouble was, a man's libido didn't abide by logic, especially not when another equally solid fact was that the woman he hankered for had looked devastated when he'd cut the evening short. He wasn't the only one with more on his mind than finding a missing baby!

So who was he fooling? And how long was he going to wait before he made his move?

She'd been brushing her teeth and still had the brush in her hand when she answered his knock. When she saw who her visitor was, her eyes flew wide and her mouth formed a perfect pink O of surprise.

"You shouldn't be opening your door without checking to see who's on the other side, cookie," he said. "Even in a hotel as fine as this, you never know who might be roaming the halls."

"I thought you were the maid, come to turn down the bed," she stammered, clutching her thin cotton robe tightly to her breasts as if she feared they might fly out and attack him.

"Sorry if I've disappointed you."

"I didn't say that." She swallowed, jittery as a kitten confronting a coyote. "Why have you come back?"

"To say good night."

"You already did."

"No, cookie. Not the way I wanted to."

"And how was that?" she said, wiping surreptitiously at a dribble of toothpaste inching down her chin.

His gaze followed her movement. Settled on her very sexy, delicious mouth. "Well, it struck me that there's one part of this husband-wife act that we forgot to practice, and we do want to give a convincing performance tomorrow, don't we?"

"That's probably a good idea." She hovered on the threshold, nervously shifting her balance from one foot to the other. "I don't fancy being exposed as an impostor."

"I didn't think you would." He stepped nearer. "Newlyweds tend to be very demonstrative, you know," he said, lowering his head until his lips grazed hers. "They do this a lot."

"Ohh!" she sighed, her mouth melting under his.

By her own admission, she'd had little experience where sex was concerned, but the way she responded to a kiss was erotic enough to send a man's resistance threshold shooting right off the chart.

Hazily aware of the musical ding-dong of the elevator doors sliding open, of the sound of voices approaching down the hall, he held her away enough to mutter hoarsely, "It's a bit public out here, even for a married couple."

A delicate flush tinted her cheeks. She lowered her eyes modestly. "Then perhaps you'd better come inside."

"I thought you'd never ask," he said, swinging her off

her feet and accepting the invitation before she had second thoughts.

He kicked the door shut behind him, lowered her to the floor slowly so that she slithered the length of him, an inch at a time, then kissed her again. At length. Thoroughly.

"That's better," he said, lifting his head finally and smacking his lips experimentally. "A much more fitting end to the evening. I'll sleep better now."

"But it doesn't have to end here, does it?"

He regarded her intently, gave her a moment to retract the question. Interpreting his silence as a brush-off, she turned her face aside and pressed her hands to her flaming cheeks. "Forget I said that. I didn't mean it the way it sounded."

"Then how did you mean it, Linda?"

"Why do you do that?" she cried, wheeling away.

"Do what?"

"You only ever call me Linda when something momentous occurs, or when I've done something to annoy you," she cried distractedly. "And you *always* say my name in your police voice!"

"Police voice?" He had to bite his lips to keep from laughing out loud.

She retreated to the other side of the bed. "With the kind of stern authority that tolerates no prevaricating!"

"I see." Following her, he said, "In that case, *Linda*, answer the question, and never mind fibbing. Exactly what did you mean when you said the evening doesn't have to end here?"

Still she tried to dodge the truth. "I'm not sure, exactly. We could have a nightcap, maybe? Go over our strategy for tomorrow one last time?"

"Or we could pick up where we left off last night. Isn't that what you really want to say? And never mind giving me the big innocent eyes, darlin'," he said, corralling her between the window and an armchair. "I wasn't born yesterday. I'm a grown man who knows when a woman's interested in more than the pleasure of my scintillating conversation.''

''Well, you might be a grown man, but you're certainly no gentleman!''

''And how do you arrive at that conclusion?''

Once again, she wriggled out of his arms. ''By recognizing that only a boor would force a woman to beg him to make love to her. And quit stalking me like this!''

He snagged her around the waist and drew her inexorably back to him. ''Is that what you're doing, Linda? Begging me to make love to you? Because if you're sure that's what you want, darlin', I'm definitely gentleman enough to oblige.''

''Don't do me any favors! I've waited twenty-eight years to find out if sex is all it's cracked up to be. I can wait a bit longer.''

''It isn't a question of favors,'' he said. ''It's a question of your being sure you know what you're doing. We went through a bottle of wine with dinner tonight—''

''Are you suggesting I'm drunk?''

''No,'' he said. ''You don't taste of alcohol, you taste of toothpaste. Again. And I must be some sort of fool to be suffering another attack of scruples when making love to you was exactly what I had in mind when I came knocking on your door.''

''Well, then,'' she said, on an impatient sigh, ''will you please stop talking about it, and just get on with it?''

He needed no second invitation. Unlike last night, this time he was prepared. The conditions were right: a bed, music drifting from the radio, chilled champagne in the courtesy bar, the streetlights throwing a soft glow over the ceiling and cloaking the rest of the room in subtle shadows. No chance they'd be interrupted. And the rest of the night to show her what she'd been missing all these years.

''Sure,'' he murmured, kissing her eyelids as he molded her to him just enough to reassure her of how willing he was to cooperate. ''I'd probably have made my move sooner if it weren't that you mentioned once that you've never been with a man before.''

"Actually," she said, turning pink. "That's only partly true."

"Partly?" He reared back, the better to see if she was having him on. But she looked perfectly serious. "I don't think it works that way, cookie. Either you have or you haven't." He tilted her face up so that she had to look him in the eye. "Not that it matters one way or the other, you understand. But if I *am* the only one, I'd like to know beforehand. Your first time should be special."

"Well…I almost let a man make love to me once when I lived in Italy. But, at the last minute, it didn't work out."

"In other words, you've never actually—?" He stopped, at a loss to phrase the question delicately.

"I probably would have, but he…couldn't. He tried, but…'' She glanced away, her color deepening, and he wondered if she had any idea how fascinated he was by the blush of innocence underlying her otherwise sophisticated demeanor. "I think he went suddenly impotent," she whispered, looking around furtively as if she feared the room might be bugged.

"I see." Cupping her cheek, he forced her to meet his gaze again. "That's not going to happen if we make love tonight, Linda. When you wake up in the morning, there won't be any question about whether or not you're still a virgin. I want you to be very clear about that. And very sure you're ready to deal with the consequences of your decision."

"If you mean contraception—"

"No." He patted the pocket containing the condom. "That's my responsibility. I'm talking about the emotional fallout."

"I won't ask you if you'll respect me in the morning, if that's what's worrying you."

"The important thing is that you respect yourself."

"I do—and will." A spark of mischief lit up her face. "Tell me, Mac, is all this talking what they call foreplay?"

"Yeah," he said, returning her smile. "But we're ready to progress to the more interesting part now, and we're going to take our time with it, darlin', because some things shouldn't be rushed."

He'd never made love to a half-virgin before, and he wanted to do it right. Make it as close to perfect for her as possible. Wipe away all memory of her first disappointing foray into sex, and leave her instead with memories she'd treasure for the rest of her life. So he began slowly, coaxing her to respond to his touch, to touch him back.

She still wore her bra and panties under the robe. Rippled silk edged with baby-fine lace the color of pale yellow roses. Little bits of things designed less to cover a woman than to drive her man crazy. He had to discipline himself not to handle the dainty fabric too roughly. To remember that she was just as fine, just as delicate.

"You're beautiful," he whispered, dipping his tongue into her ear, and felt her tremble.

"I'm ordinary," she replied, squeezing her eyes shut as he tasted the curve of her throat.

He unhooked the fastener on her bra, slipped the straps down her arms, and tossed the garment to the floor. "You're perfect."

And she was. Skin as smooth and cool as cream. Breasts small and firm. Waist so narrow he could span it with his hands.

Better not dwell too long on the rest of her, not if he wanted to prolong her pleasure. And pleasing her he was. Her pulse was racing, her breathing increasingly labored. When he took her nipple in his mouth and tugged gently, she let out a helpless moan.

Count to a hundred, Sullivan, he cautioned, feeling his command of the situation slip alarmingly as she pulled his shirt free from the waist of his pants and ran her hands over the contours of his bare chest.

He got as far as fifteen before conceding a battle lost before it started. She might be a novice in the art of love, but she was also a natural, and a very quick study. For every inroad he made on her control, she returned the favor in full measure.

"This might not last as long as I'd hoped," he said hoarsely, as he removed the last of her underthings. She was all sweetly exposed curves flung into gold relief by the glow of the city lights, and dusky shadows begging to be discovered.

She hooked a finger inside his belt. "Shall I speed things up?" she asked, and without waiting for him to answer, began peeling away his clothes, a layer at a time.

"Ohh!" she breathed, staring at him in unfeigned awe when at last he stood before her, buck naked and at full standing alert. "I knew you'd be…impressive, but I had no idea you were quite this magnificent."

She moistened her lips with the tip of her tongue, a mannerism made all the more erotic because it was so ingenuous. Or was it? Was he the naive one here, and she the expert? Because the way she paralleled the action by drawing her fingertip the full-length of his mightily engorged flesh just about brought him to climax, and that wasn't part of his master plan.

"Oh, no, you don't! Not yet," he panted, rescuing himself from attack by backing her toward the bed and when she fell onto the mattress, pinning her hands above her head to prevent her inflicting more torture.

And then, with her trembling and submissive beneath him, he had his way with her. At leisure. Feasting on the sight and feel and taste of her. Reveling in the helpless moans interspersed with gasps, which she couldn't suppress. Exulting as she quivered and writhed when he found her with his tongue.

Finally, with his own fortitude so seriously under siege that she had to help him put on the condom, he slid inside her in a rush of heat and sensation that made a mockery of s notion that he was in charge of anything, least of all mself. He'd have laughed at his own arrogance if he'd ssessed the wherewithal to do anything other than obey e dictates of primal instinct. The best he could do was ld her fast as they hurtled toward the brink of insanity en, when there was no avoiding its rapacious demands, ee-falling with her beyond the realm of everything that pt him grounded in reality.

He'd expected to bring her to orgasm, and she did not sappoint him, or herself. What he didn't expect was how eply he would be affected by her experience. He'd had ough women to know the difference between a fake per- rmance and the real thing, and Linda's response had been nuine.

He'd recognized the distant tremors gathering strength ithin her, heard the inarticulate cry torn from her as she etered on the brink of completion, felt the involuntary enching of her flesh around his as she climaxed. But that was so puffed up with pride at having been the one to duce her response—*that* was a first, and he didn't have e vaguest idea how to deal with it.

It was only sex, after all. A man and a woman mutually volved in the giving and taking of physical pleasure, and the firm understanding that any emotional fallout was as mporary as the thrill of orgasm itself.

So where was all this mushy sentiment coming from? It asn't his style at all, and he hadn't the first clue what to about it.

What he *did* know was that he needed to get out of there, fore he said something he'd regret in the morning. But e'd curled up next to him, all warm and rosy and smelling woman and sex. Leaving her and braving the air- nditioned solitude of his own room held no appeal at all.

He'd wait until she was asleep. Possibly nap a little him- lf. The important thing was to keep his mouth shut and member he'd brought only one condom with him.

* * *

The Wagners lived on Russian Hill, in an Italianate jewe of a house sitting in a long, narrow garden full of splashir fountains and flowers.

Jackson the butler, immaculate in pin-striped dinner sui met them at the door, eyed them up and down to make su they were fit company for his employers and allowed the entry.

"I feel I should have worn a tux," Mac murmured, they followed him up a flight of stairs and through a doub parlor to the sun-drenched terrace.

"You look perfectly all right," Linda said, controllir the urge to wax eloquent over his appearance. His light gra suit was clearly custom tailored, his white shirt of the fine Egyptian cotton, his tie pure silk. Even in a city as sophis ticated as San Francisco, there were few men, she was sur who came close to rivaling the ease and elegance wit which he carried himself.

"You don't look so bad yourself. Is that dress new, did you bring it with you?"

"I bought it this morning." *After I woke up and foun you gone. After I ate breakfast alone, because the messag you left said you had some business to take care of an wouldn't be back until after lunch.*

"It was a good choice. I like that blue-green color o you. It does things for your eyes."

Things? "Thank you," she said, demurely.

"How's the ring? Not leaving any black marks on yo finger, I hope."

"No." She touched it lightly, fondly, still amazed tha he'd had the foresight to think of buying it. The diamant studded wedding band might not be any more real than th marriage it symbolized and would probably turn green i time, but to her, it represented the magic and enthrallme of last night, and she would treasure it forever.

"Mr. and Mrs. Sullivan, madam," Jackson announce grandly, stepping to one side as a woman in her mid-fifti rose from a wicker chaise to greet them.

She was slim, elegant and discreetly expensive in a flowing silk dress patterned all over with tiny violets. She was also charming. "How do you do?" she said, her voice a well-modulated blend of culture and breeding. "I'm so pleased you contacted us. Won't you sit down? My husband's been called to the telephone but he'll join us shortly."

She gestured to a wicker love seat, which matched her chaise. "I thought we'd gather here in the garden, since it's such a lovely evening. Do you know San Francisco well?"

Mac said, "Yes. I've spent a lot of time here in the past."

"Not well at all, I'm afraid. This is our first visit," Linda announced simultaneously, and turned to him, stricken at having committed such a faux pas this early in the game.

"What my wife means," he said easily, taking her hand, "is that this is her inaugural visit as well as our first as a married couple."

"So you're newlyweds!" Mrs. Wagner smiled warmly. "I should have guessed from the way you look at each other. Are you on your honeymoon, by chance?"

"In a way, yes," Mac said. The way he crushed Linda's hand in his sent a clear message that she should keep her mouth shut. "We've been married such a short time that every day's another honeymoon."

"How wonderful! I remember feeling exactly the same when James and I were first married, and I can't say things have changed all that much over the years." She glanced up and broke into another smile as a tall, frail man leaning heavily on a cane came out of the house to join them. "Your ears must be burning," she told him. "I was just talking about you. Darling, this is Mr. and Mrs. Sullivan from Vancouver, although you, Mr. Sullivan, sound more American than Canadian."

"I'm from Oregon," he said, rising to shake James Wagner's hand, "but we're staying in Vancouver temporarily, until things return to normal with my wife's family."

Mr. Wagner offered Linda an old-world bow before lowering himself carefully onto a straight-backed chair. "That sounds ominous. No trouble on the home front, I trust?"

"Oh, surely not!" Mrs. Wagner exclaimed. "Darling, this young couple are newlyweds, enjoying an extended honeymoon, and I think we should have champagne to celebrate. After all, the bride is June's sister, which makes her practically related to us."

"Then by all means, let's have champagne. Jackson, bring up a bottle of Taittinger, will you?"

For the next twenty minutes, they sipped wine and made small talk. Eventually, though, when the atmosphere was all nice and mellow, Mac got down to business. "I think it's only fair to tell you that this isn't entirely a social visit. There is trouble, just as you suspected, Mr. Wagner, and we're hoping you can help us resolve it."

James Wagner might have been feeble in body, but there was nothing wrong with his mind. He picked up on the grim delivery of such news at once, and regarded Mac sharply. "It's to do with that bounder of a son of ours, isn't it?"

"I'm afraid it is, sir."

"I should have known!" He thumped his cane on the flagstone terrace. "Sadie and I have been uneasy about him for months now. Has he run off and left your sister in the lurch, Mrs. Sullivan? Is that what this is all about?"

Linda glanced at Mac, wishing the question had been addressed to him. He squeezed her fingers again, this time more in encouragement than warning. "Actually my sister is the one who called off the wedding," she said, unsure how much she should reveal.

"Smart girl!" Kirk's father decreed. "But there's more, isn't there?"

Again, she looked to Mac for guidance. "Go ahead, Linda," he said. "Tell them about the baby."

"Dear heaven!" Mrs. Wagner exclaimed. "Has something happened to our granddaughter? Is that why Kirk hasn't been in touch for so long?"

"I'm afraid he's run away with her," Linda said, wishing

there was a kinder way to put it. "You're not the only ones who haven't heard from him, Mrs. Wagner. No one seems to know where he is or how to get in touch with him."

Ashen-faced, the poor woman turned to her husband. "Oh, James! What does this mean?"

"You might as well face it, Sadie. If what these people are telling us is true, our son's living on the wrong side of the law. Isn't that right, Mr. Sullivan?"

"I'm afraid it is."

Mrs. Wagner raised her hands to her face as if warding off a blow. "No, there must be some mistake! We brought Kirk up to know the difference between right and wrong. He's just taken the baby to show her off to friends. He might even be bringing her here to see us. He'll turn up again soon, don't you think, Mr. Sullivan?"

"I very much doubt it," Mac said. "To put it bluntly, he's kidnapped his own child."

"Well, he has to be caught and held accountable," James Wagner declared. "How long has he been gone?"

Linda exchanged glances with Mac, and at his nod, said, "Nearly two months. He took Angela when she was one day old."

The high color in Mr. Wagner's face faded to sickly yellow. Clearly shaken, he said, "Do we even know if that child is still alive?"

"No. The police have found no trace of him or the baby," Mac said.

"So you're conducting your own search. That's why you're really here, isn't it?"

Mac nodded. "Yes, sir, it is. We're hoping you might have some idea where he might be hiding."

"Not here, if that's what you're thinking," Mr. Wagner maintained, spots of anger staining his cheeks a dull red. "He knows better than to expect we'd give him refuge for something like this! How is your poor sister holding up under the stress, Mrs. Sullivan?"

"Not well," Linda said, her delight at being taken for

Mac's wife evaporating. Beyond doubt, the Wagners were as distressed about what had happened as anyone else, and it left a very bad taste in her mouth to be heaping deceit on top of the pain they already suffered.

"She must be nearly mad with anxiety!"

"More than you can imagine," Mac said, slipping his arm around Linda's shoulders and pulling her snugly against him. "Everyone's worried, of course, but it's hardest on the mother when a child goes missing."

Still beside herself, Mrs. Wagner appealed to her husband. "It's happened again, hasn't it, James?"

Linda felt the sudden tension running through Mac and wasn't surprised when he leaned forward and said, "Why would you even ask such a question, Mrs. Wagner? Has he done this before?"

She rounded on him, clearly offended. "No, of course not! Kirk is not a criminal!"

But Mac pressed on, undeterred. "Then what did you mean? What do you know that you're not telling us?"

"He's been...unwell, in the past."

"Unwell how?"

She fidgeted with the collar of her dress. "He's gone through periods of...mental instability and required...therapy. But he's quite recovered."

"No, he's not. If he's run off with a baby, he's off his rocker!" James Wagner thundered. "Stop trying to make excuses for the man, Sadie! We've been dealing with problems of one kind or another since the day Kirk came into our lives. He was trouble from the very first."

"And I spoiled him. You said that from the first, too, James, and warned me I'd live to regret it," she cried, unraveling before their eyes. "And I suppose you think it's my fault he's—"

"Your son is a grown man," Mac told her gently. "He's the one responsible for the trouble he's now in, not you. One thing does puzzle me, though. Until we told you about the baby, you didn't appear to find it odd that Kirk hadn't remained in contact with you, and I wonder why that is, when you're so obviously devoted to him.''

Mr. Wagner let out a sharp bark of a laugh. ''You wouldn't, if you knew Kirk! We'll go months without a word from him, and then, out of the blue, he'll show up on the doorstep and act as if we'd last seen him just the day before.''

''And you never asked him why?''

''Certainly we asked, young man! But that doesn't mean we received answers that made sense. Kirk has always been secretive. To give you an idea of what I'm talking about, he was only eight when he asked for a lock to be put on his bedroom door to keep everyone else out—something to which I was vehemently opposed, by the way.''

''But I let him have one,'' Mrs. Wagner said, on a painful breath. ''I hoped it would show him that we respected his need for privacy.''

''You tried to accommodate him his entire life, Sadie, and never once got a sincere word of thanks for your efforts!''

''He always found it hard to trust people, that was the problem,'' she said, dabbing her eyes with a dainty handkerchief. ''He was insecure from the very start. It had to do with his being adopted, I believe. As soon as he was old enough, he became obsessed with finding his birth family, and even changed his name because he said we weren't his real parents. It broke my heart that he didn't realize how much we loved him.''

Mr. Wagner banged his cane again. ''Well, I won't put up with his doing it again. Mrs. Sullivan, I'm grieved and ashamed that a son of mine is causing your family such heartache. Be assured you may count on our cooperation in holding him answerable for his actions.''

''Will he go to prison when he's caught, Mr. Sullivan?'' Sadie asked fearfully.

''That'll be up to the authorities and the family. A good deal depends on what happens next. If he were to return the baby voluntarily to her mother, it's possible that lesser charges could be brought against him.'' Mac stood up and drew Linda to her feet also. "I'm afraid we've spoiled your evening. I'm sorry we had to be the ones to bring you such distressing news.''

"Yes," Linda said, wishing they hadn't bothered coming at all, since the only thing they'd done was draw two more innocent people into the mess. "Thank you very much for seeing us."

Both Wagners rose also. "We haven't been much help, I'm afraid," Sadie said. "I hope you'll keep us informed, though. We might not be blood relatives, but that little baby holds a very special place in our hearts. We so hoped she would bring Kirk the peace and satisfaction he didn't find in his first marriage.''

"He'll never find it with anyone," Mr. Wagner growled. "He's not interested in making a life with someone else. All he's ever wanted is to own and control people. It's what drove away his ex-wife and it's why this second marriage never took place.''

"We'll be in touch as soon as we know something ourselves." Mac reached into his inside jacket pocket and extracted a business card. "Meanwhile, if you happen to think of something which might help locate him—someplace he might use as a refuge, for example—you can reach us at any of these numbers.''

Linda thought that was the end of it; that for all their earlier optimism that the Wagners would provide the answers they needed, they'd come up empty-handed. In fact, she and Mac had reached the head of the stairs where the butler Jackson waited to show them out, when James Wagner's voice stopped them cold.

"Wait a minute! I just thought of something. Maybe we know more than we first thought.''

CHAPTER TEN

"WELL, that was a telling encounter in more ways than one! Who'd have thought we'd strike gold just when we were ready to abandon the mine?" Reflection of the yellow candle flame danced in Mac's eyes as he regarded Linda across the table.

"Do you really think we have?"

"With an out-of-the-way vacation home, which the Wagners haven't used in years, and to which Thayer's got the keys? You bet! This calls for a celebration. Can you stand another round of champagne?"

She shrugged, her attempt to match his cheerful enthusiasm falling short. "If you like."

"You'd rather have something else?"

"No. Champagne is fine."

"Then what's the problem? This place isn't to your liking? You don't see anything you fancy on the menu? The wine list's not extensive enough?"

Anything but! The supper club he'd chosen was first-class all the way, from its scenic location on the water, just a few blocks from Fisherman's Wharf, to the well-appointed fixtures and excellent but unobtrusive service. To be seated by the window, at a table with a centerpiece of fresh bud roses around a silver candleholder, across from a man she was falling for in a big way, should have been enough to make for a perfect romantic evening. Would have been, were it not for the niggling questions clouding her mind.

"Okay, Linda." He snapped his fingers impatiently. "Out with it. Why the long face?"

"I'm trying to decide between pheasant and crab cakes."

145

"And?" He tilted his handsome head to one side. "Something else is bugging you, and as your husband-for-a-day, I demand to know what it is."

"Well, for a start, I'm wondering why you insisted on perpetuating the lie that we're married to a sweet old couple like the Wagners who were clearly shattered to learn what Kirk's done."

"Because we agreed beforehand that a measure of deception was necessary."

"I know. I just wish that, once we realized they were on our side, you'd let me tell them the truth, instead of racing me to the car and driving off while I still had one leg practically dragging on the road!"

"It was a harmless but necessary pretense."

"I've never been very good at pretense, harmless or otherwise. I prefer to be up-front in my dealings with people."

He propped his elbow on the arm of his chair and surveyed her thoughtfully. "Don't you think they'd been disillusioned enough for one day? They must be in their seventies, and neither struck me as being particularly robust. You saw how unglued Sadie became when she learned what Thayer's been up to, and as for the old man, for all his tough talk, he looks as if a good wind might blow him away. I could see no advantage to adding insult to the injury they'd already sustained."

"I thought it might be that you didn't trust them."

For once, his gaze wasn't quite as direct as usual. "Let's just say I prefer to temper optimism with caution. The Wagners are probably on the level. James, in particular, has had it up to here with Thayer."

"And Sadie?"

He made a face. "Is a loose cannon. She might give us trouble without meaning to."

"What makes you think that?"

"Because, first and foremost, she's a mother who's spent years trying to protect and please her only child whom she obviously worships, regardless of how often he's screwed

up. It would be a mistake to assume she'll abandon him
now when he's in the worst trouble of his miserable life—
which is another reason not to tell her that we're not everything we pretended to be. It doesn't pay to get careless,
especially not at this stage of the game. Time enough for
true confessions when Angela's back with her mother,
where she belongs.''

"I hope you're right.''

"No question about it,'' he said cheerfully, flagging
down their server. "So kick back and enjoy your dinner
date with a clear conscience, Mrs. Sullivan. You've earned
a night on the town.''

But would it end with dinner and champagne? she wondered, peeking at him from behind her menu as he discussed
the wine list with the waiter. Or had their lovemaking meant
enough to him that he wanted to repeat the experiment?

Glancing up suddenly, he caught her spying and favored
her with a slow wink. Feeling a blush burn her cheeks and
afraid he'd recognize the naked desire she was sure showed
in her eyes, she buried her face in the menu again.

How quickly a relationship could blossom, just when a
person was ready to give up on its ever bearing fruit! She'd
never expected to find him outside her door a second time
last night, and hadn't lied when she'd told him she thought
it was someone from housekeeping.

The Hyatt, though, didn't hire maids who stood well over
six feet tall and who sported a five-o'clock shadow. Nor
did such employees have voices registering a full two oc-
taves below middle C. Only Mac Sullivan filled that description, and only Mac Sullivan could turn her weak at the
knees with a single glance. Those stormy eyes could cut
like a laser on occasion, as she very well knew, but they'd
blazed with caressing warmth as he'd stripped away her
clothing and run his hands over her naked body.

"That suit you, Linda?''

She blinked and found him and the waiter regarding her
expectantly. "I'm sorry. Does what suit me?''

"Crab cakes as an appetizer and pheasant for the main course."

"Oh! Oh, yes. Absolutely."

"You were doing it again, cookie," he scolded, after the waiter left with their order. "I could practically hear the wheels spinning in your head. So what's on your mind now?"

She shrugged and tried to pass off her insatiable need for reassurance as nothing more than mild interest. "I was just thinking about last night."

"Pretty memorable, huh?"

"Pretty astonishing, actually." She took a sip of water to give herself time to choose her next words carefully. It wouldn't do to come across as too needy. "I didn't think you were interested in me in…that way."

"I've been interested for quite some time, and if you hadn't already picked up on that, I must be losing my touch."

But how interested? she longed to ask him. *Just-for-one-night interested, or have we embarked on something more lasting?* But men smelled obligation and entrapment in such questions, and the last thing she wanted was to send him running for the hills. So, "No chance of that," she said. "You made it very special for me."

It? What an inept, pathetic word to apply to the most wonderful experience of her life!

"Thank you," he said, with what struck her as altogether too much self-satisfaction. "I like to think I'm tuned in to a woman's needs enough to be able to satisfy her."

A woman? How about *this* woman, Mac? The one sitting opposite you now, wearing the dress you professed to admire—not to mention perfume at two hundred and fifty dollars an ounce and a hairdo that cost just about the same!—and doing her best to impress upon you that she's different from the rest of the herd? More to the point, how would you like it if I thought of you in terms of just *a man?*

"Not that I have much experience on which to base an opinion," she replied loftily, "but I'd say you were..."

"Yes?" He grinned and reached for her hand.

She snatched it away. "Adequate."

There! Stick that in your studly pipe and smoke it!

He compressed his lips, as if he were having a hard time not laughing in her face. "In that case, why does thinking about it leave you looking like the cat which didn't quite manage to swallow the canary?"

"It doesn't," she said, having no trouble blithely disregarding the truth in this instance. "I happen to be enjoying myself very much."

"You could have fooled me."

"Perhaps because I find my attention wandering from the relatively trivial subject of your sexual proficiency to more imperative issues."

"Ouch!" He slapped his cheek smartly. "Take that, Sullivan, you arrogant, conceited pig, and get your mind out of the gutter! The lady has 'issues' on her mind."

She glared at him, beyond exasperated.

"Watch it," he cautioned, clearly having a whale of a good time at her expense. "Fulminating in public can land you in serious trouble with the law!"

She wished she could shrug off her insecurity and retaliate in kind. Laugh with him and play the man-woman game with a carefree heart. But she couldn't. He mattered too much. And to her horror, instead of returning his frivolous banter, a lump rose in her throat and her eyes swam with sudden tears.

"Do you suppose," she gulped, "that you could be serious for a minute, and tell me honestly if what we learned from the Wagners will prove useful?"

"Hey, cookie, I'm teasing you, okay?" He trapped her left hand and stroked the bogus wedding ring gently.

"Just answer the question."

"It's definitely worth looking into."

"So what do we do next?"

"We pay a visit to Catalina Island." Releasing her hand, he leaned back in his chair and waited until their server had poured the wine before continuing, "I think there's a very good chance we'll find him holed up there. We know the house is set in private grounds, high in the hills above Avalon Bay, which makes it a perfect hideaway."

"From the way the Wagners described it, it sounds perfectly gorgeous. I wonder why they don't use it anymore?"

"There are hardly any cars on the island so people either use golf carts to get around, or they walk. From what we saw this afternoon, it's my guess James would find the exercise more of a cardiac challenge than he could manage. We had a bit of a chat while you were saying goodbye to Sadie, and if it were up to him, he'd sell the place and invest the money elsewhere. But she inherited it from her mother and wants to hang on to it for sentimental reasons. So it pretty well stands empty year-round, except for a skeleton staff who look after it."

"Then Kirk would feel relatively safe there."

"Absolutely. No one would question his right to move in, and from all accounts, the house is far enough away from neighbors to give the kind of privacy he craves and needs. Plus, there's a twenty-mile stretch of water between him and the mainland, which increases his chances of going undiscovered, especially in the summer when the island's crammed with tourists."

"My intuition tells me that's where he's hiding."

"Mine says it's time for a toast." He clinked the rim of his glass lightly against hers. "So here's to my make-believe wife for a job well-done. You handled yourself like a pro today, cookie."

"Here's to my make-believe husband."

"We make quite a pair." His gaze roamed over her, lingering warmly at her breasts, her throat, her face.

The champagne sparkled over her tongue. "Yes." *Oh, yes!*

It was probably a good thing that the waiter brought their

crab cakes just then, or dear only knew what foolish things she might have said.

"Well?" Mac inquired lazily, watching as she sampled the food. "Does it meet your gourmet standards?"

"Very much so. This is an excellent restaurant."

"It's always been one of my favorites."

A vague chill of uneasiness slithered over her. "So this isn't your first visit?"

"No." He gave a casual shrug. "I've been here several times before."

With other women?

Don't ask, Linda!

"I guess I shouldn't be surprised," she said, doing her utmost to match his nonchalance. "You did mention to the Wagners that you're familiar with San Francisco and visit quite often."

"I have friends here. You want to dance, cookie?"

She'd been hoping he'd elaborate on the friends, but dancing with him promised much greater satisfaction. "I'd love to."

He clasped her hand and led her to a small area at the far end of the club where several other couples swayed to a musical quartet's smoochy rendition of "I Left My Heart In San Francisco."

"Corny but nice," Mac said, drawing her into his arms.

"You mean me, or the song?"

He laughed down at her and settled his hand more firmly in the small of her back. "I can think of better words to describe you."

"Such as?"

"Pretty, desirable, smart."

She closed her eyes, the better to savor the compliment, and the way their bodies moved together in perfect sync as if they'd danced together for years. She loved the possessive way he held her, as if she belonged to him. She loved his aftershave, the slightly rough texture of his fingers wrapped around hers.

Ye gods, she might as well admit it: she loved all of him!

Was she crazy? Some might think so. But she knew otherwise. Had known, the second she set eyes on him, that he was different from any other man she'd ever met and that he would impact her life in a very big way.

She stirred in his arms. "Do you believe in fate, Mac?"

She'd barely voiced the question when the dance band segued into "Santa Catalina." "Cripes!" Mac said, almost stepping on her toes. "If I didn't before, I do now! Talk about uncanny coincidence!"

"It's a good omen," she murmured, allowing her hand to steal around his neck. "We're going to find Angela and take her home. I feel it in my bones."

"Yes, we are," he agreed, suddenly ushering her off the dance floor. "But first, we're going to enjoy tonight, beginning with Pheasant Supreme. Our waiter just delivered dinner."

She heard unspoken promise in his tone; a pledge of something more than the meal awaiting them. She sensed it in the touch of his hands stroking intimately down her arms as he seated her at their table, and again in the way his gaze remained connected to hers as he took his place opposite. But more than the physical awareness, she felt a less tangible connection between them, one which left the very air vibrating with electricity.

Did he feel it, too? The question hovered on her lips, itching to be set free. Yearning to capture him. But another voice intervened; a stranger's voice, light, charming, and utterly feminine. "Mac, my old friend, I hoped I'd run into you here."

He looked up and, at the sight of the woman poised like an exotic butterfly next to their table, broke into a smile of such warmth that Linda flinched from the heat of it.

"Hey, sweet face!" he crooned, throwing down his napkin and leaping up from his chair to envelop her in a hug.

"Penny told me you'd stopped by the shop this mornng,'' she said, kissing him. ''Why didn't you let me know ahead of time you were coming to town?''

''It was a last-minute decision.'' He held her at arm's length, oozing approval and admiration. ''You're looking wonderful, as always.''

She gurgled with laughter, a musical ripple of delight. ''You're not so bad yourself, Detective!''

''Why, thank you, ma'am.''

Arm locked around her tiny waist, he continued to gaze at her, oblivious to anyone else in the room. But she, at least, had the good manners to pull away and acknowledge Linda.

''Hi, I'm Andrea, and you must think I'm dreadfully rude, barging in on your dinner like this.''

''Oh, right, you haven't met!'' Mac banged the heel of his hand to his forehead, as if to juggle his brain into remembering the name of the dumpling in the turquoise dress who sat there with a sickly, self-conscious smile pasted on her face. ''This is...my client, Linda Carr.''

His client! Or, to state it more accurately, the afterthought he wished would disappear in a puff of smoke, and never mind that he'd been rolling around in bed with her just the night before!

''Ah, the acting Mrs. Sullivan!'' Andrea exclaimed without a shred of malice, and gestured to Linda's left hand. ''How does the ring fit?''

''Quite well, thank you.''

''And it did the job? You passed yourself off successfully as Mac's wife?''

''It appears so.'' She forced herself to try to reciprocate the other woman's buoyant good humor. ''Fortunately it's a temporary arrangement.''

Andrea threw back her perfectly coiffed auburn head and set forth with another infectious bubble of laughter. ''Just as well! But if he's not the ideal husband, he's certainly the best man you could have working for you.'' She touched

Linda's hand briefly, sympathetically. "He'll make sure everything works out, you'll see."

"I hope so."

"Me, too, Linda. You'll be in my thoughts." She straightened and turned again to Mac. "Sorry we missed each other this morning. I'd have loved to meet for lunch. Can we do it tomorrow instead?"

"Doubtful," he said, bathing her in that warmly encompassing smile again. "We'll likely be heading south about then."

A little moue of disappointment crossed her lovely face.

"Breakfast, then? At my place? We can make it early." She batted her eyelashes in blatant bribery. "I'll make your favorite."

"With strawberries?"

"Yes, you brat. And whipped cream, too." She peered over her shoulder at Linda. "You're welcome to join us, if you like."

And witness more of their billing and cooing, not to mention the way they couldn't keep their hands off each other? She'd never keep her food down! "I don't think so, thanks."

"You could have made more of an effort to be gracious," Mac rebuked, resuming his seat as Andrea floated away on a cloud of black chiffon.

"I was perfectly polite."

"You were perfectly po-faced!"

"I'm surprised you noticed. It seemed to me you didn't have eyes for anyone but your girlfriend."

"She's not my girlfriend."

"Oh, really!" The careless laugh she aimed for emerged as an outraged squawk, the result, no doubt, of the acid taint of jealousy burning holes in her throat. "Your mistress, then?"

"No. My ex-wife."

She should have known! The way Andrea had fingered

the hair back from his brow, the kiss she'd dropped just beside his mouth, had screamed familiarity, possession.

Linda had feared there might be a price to pay for stealing a night of pure, undiluted pleasure in the midst of so much angst, and now she knew what it was: the emergence of this beautiful, gracious, compassionate woman, her concern for a stranger so sincere that it slipped with the ease of stiletto blade between Linda's ribs and crucified her.

For some men, one woman is never enough.... Mac's words rang through her memory like a death knell. But the other side of that coin surely was that, for other men, there was only ever one woman.

Death's the only barrier to repairing a relationship, he'd said, and she hadn't believed him at the time. But she did now. She'd seen the evidence firsthand.

Her stomach heaved and she clapped a hand to her mouth, sure she was going to be sick. Thank God she hadn't told him how she felt about him, or worse yet, asked him if he returned her feelings, even though they'd known each other only a few days! Because time was relative when it came to love, and it had taken mere seconds for her to realize he was still besotted with his ex-wife, and all the rest—the flirtation, the occasional tenderness, the *sex with her, his client!*—had meant nothing!

"Why the horrified expression, Linda?" he asked coldly. "You've known all along that I'm divorced."

"Yes," she said. "And after seeing the two of you together just now, I can't help but wonder why you bothered to end the marriage."

He regarded her over the rim of his glass. "You need to get over the notion that divorced couples have to be at each other's throats all the time. It's not like that for your mother and father, whether or not you're willing to admit it, and it's not like that for Andrea and me. Relationships are seldom that black and white, my dear."

"Please don't lecture me as if I were a child! I'm fully

aware that some divorced couples are able to remain friends.''

"No, you're not," he said flatly. "You're furious. Why is that, Linda? Could it be that you're jealous?"

Of a gorgeous wisp of a woman in black chiffon, who made him glow with delight and who was still on such intimate terms with him that she entertained him at *her place?* "Certainly not!"

"That's good," he said silkily. "Because you'd be seriously out of line, if you were. Just because you're paying me to find your niece doesn't make me your personal property."

"I'm not paying you to be chasing your ex-wife all over town, either."

"She designs costume jewelry. You needed a ring. Who else would I have gone to, to supply one?"

What was the matter with her? Where was her legendary common sense, the one thing she'd always been able to count on when faced with a dilemma? She knew better than to let her emotions run away with her like this, for heaven's sake, especially over a man she barely knew—and especially over one who, even before she met him, she'd been warned was a loner and a maverick.

It was all the champagne's fault! That, and the enchantment of the setting. As darkness fell, lamplight from the boats moored in the adjoining marina rippled like fireflies over the water. A hazy moon swam above the tall masts. Within the restaurant, the floor-to-ceiling windows mirrored the candle flames and flung them back in a hundred glimmering images. It was enough to make any woman lose her common sense in romantic fantasy.

But recognizing that didn't make the pain any less strident. It hammered away at her with a thousand tiny blows, even though she managed to keep it hidden. "You're quite right," she said, slipping the ring from her finger. "She was the obvious choice and if I'd known I had her to thank for supplying the props for the charade, I'd have said something when she was here. Perhaps you'd be kind enough to return this to her when you see her tomorrow.''

"Keep it," he said irritably. "She doesn't need it."

"Nor do I. It's served its purpose."

He rolled his eyes in long-suffering exasperation. "Eat your dinner and stop being such a pain in the ass, Linda!"

"I'm not hungry."

Before he could tell her what he thought of that excuse, another woman, accompanied by a man, stopped by their table. "Hello again, Mac!" she caroled. "Andrea told us you were here. What a bonus, running into you twice in one day. You remember Dave, don't you?"

"Sure. Nice to see you again, Dave." Mac stood to shake hands with the man. "Linda, this is Penny Worth, Andrea's business partner, and her fiancé, Dave Lewis."

"How do you do?" Linda said, hating that she sounded as thoroughly "po-faced" as Mac had accused her of being.

"Penny's the one who chose your ring," he informed her. "She went to quite a bit of trouble to find something she thought you'd like."

"Then I thank you." She smiled tightly. "It's lovely."

"It is pretty, isn't it? It's only ten carat gold, of course, but it's set with real Austrian crystals, so I hope you'll enjoy wearing it."

"She won't," Mac said caustically. "She feels she should return it."

"Oh, nonsense! Please keep it, if not as a memento of your visit, then as a lucky charm. Mac told me about your family's tragedy."

"Did he indeed?" Linda shot him a resentful glance.

"It must be such a trying and difficult time for you."

"Yes, it is."

Penny patted her shoulder kindly. "Thank goodness you've got Mac on your side. That swings the odds greatly in your favor, you know."

Not as much as you think, dearie! The way things are going, he's merely adding to the difficulties.

"We're all pulling for you," Dave said, his brown eyes warm with sympathy. "Listen, the reason we stopped by is to ask you both to join us for dessert. We're up on the balcony, and it's just us and Andrea and a couple of others, so you'll be among friends. Being around other people often helps at times like this."

"Sounds good," Mac said, looking offensively cheerful at the prospect of not being stuck with Linda's company for the rest of the evening. "Give us about fifteen minutes, and we'll be there."

"I don't like other people accepting invitations on my behalf, without consulting me first," she told him, the minute they were alone again.

"No?" He shrugged indifferently. "Sorry about that. It won't happen again. Anything else you'd like to get off your chest while you're at it?"

"Yes. I don't appreciate your broadcasting my private business to everyone in town."

"Stop exaggerating. I've mentioned it only to Penny, and then only in general terms. Her passing it along to her fiancé and Andrea is hardly tantamount to taking out a full page ad in the local newspaper!"

"You had no right mentioning it at all. If you were still on the police force, I could have you suspended."

"But I'm not on the police force, cookie, as you very well know. Nor did I seek you out and beg to be allowed to work for you, in case you've forgotten. So don't come the high-handed boss-lady with me, because it won't wash."

"Nevertheless, I *am* your boss. And you're fired."

"Don't be such an idiot!" He held his thumb and forefinger a quarter-inch apart. "We're this close to catching up with Thayer."

"I don't need you. Send me your bill. And don't call me 'cookie.' I've already told you I don't like it."

"You don't like me calling you 'Linda,' either, so what

would you prefer? Madam? Or will plain Ms. Carr suffice to smooth your ruffled feathers?''

She glared at him, a fresh outbreak of tears pricking her eyes. ''You are, without a doubt, the most infuriating man I've ever had the misfortune to come across.''

He closed his eyes and exhaled at length. ''Okay, let's stop this before we both say something we'll regret. Are you finished with your dinner?''

''Yes.''

''Would you like to join the people upstairs?''

''No. I'm very tired. But don't let that stop you from partying the night away. I can take a taxi back to the hotel.''

''I'll drive you.''

''No need.'' She waved the offer aside contemptuously. ''I'd hate for you to miss out on dessert.''

His lips thinned with annoyance. ''You know what? I'd hate that, too. I'll ask the hostess to call you a cab.''

''Fine. At last we're in agreement on something.''

''You're being unreasonable.''

Yes, she was! Unreasonable, childish and just plain ridiculous. And the devil of it was, she couldn't help herself! Stubbornly she stared at her hands lying clenched in her lap.

''You're treating me as if I'm the enemy, cookie.''

''Give my regrets to your friends,'' she said stonily, ''and thank them for being kind enough to include me in their plans.''

He drummed his fingers on the table and whistled under his breath. Finally he said, ''Okay, have it your way. We'll talk in the morning. Sleep well.''

''And kindly don't tell them anything else about me.''

''I'm confident we'll find other ways to keep ourselves amused.''

''Oh, I'm willing to bet they'd find the story of my impotent Italian lover very entertaining, especially if you embellish it with an account of how it took a red-blooded all-

American man like you to show me the true joys of sex,''
she cried rashly.

"Is that what's got you bent out of shape—that you
hopped in the sack with a lowly employee?" He shook his
head in disbelief. "Well, for what it's worth, Linda, I have
too much self-respect to brag about my sexual conquests.
Pity you don't hold yourself in similar esteem."

CHAPTER ELEVEN

THE morning sun flung bronze sparks through Andrea's hair and played light and shadow over her serene face. Watching as she poured coffee and passed him a cup, Mac was struck again by how different she was now from when she'd been married to him. All the sharp edges had smoothed out. She glowed with womanly contentment.

"So," he said, "are you going to marry that guy you were with last night?"

"Tom? Yes." Andrea looked at him from beneath her lashes, a cheeky smirk inching over her face. "Are you going to marry that woman you were with?"

"Hell, no!" He poked at the garland of whipped cream circling the strawberries on his Belgian waffle. "She ticks me off so much at times, I feel like putting her across my knee."

Andrea leaned back and crossed her long legs. Much longer than Linda's, he noted absently, but not quite as shapely. "In other words, she's making you nervous."

"Did I say that?"

"You didn't have to, MacKenzie. Your disquiet proclaims itself loud and clear every time her name comes up. She doesn't just tick you off, she's under your skin, big time."

"She's a client, for Pete's sake!"

"Oh, she's more than that. You're sleeping with her and wish you weren't."

"Why don't you just eat your waffle and quit trying to psychoanalyze me?" he snorted, peeved to the point that he wished he'd passed on breakfast.

"I was married to you for four years. I know you well

161

enough to recognize when you're afraid you're in deeper than you want to be—no pun intended.''

''Your imagination's running away with you, kiddo!''

''I'm right on target!'' she snorted. ''Linda Carr scares you spitless. You're afraid she's going to take up permanent residence in your sacred space.''

''I'm afraid she's reading more into our relationship than exists—and so are you.''

''But it's *your* feelings for *her* that worry you more. This woman's keeping you awake at night.'' She leaned forward and touched his cheek. ''Or are these bags under your eyes purely for decoration?''

He jerked away from her, unnerved by her insight more than he cared to admit. ''Keep this up, and I'll remember all too well why being married to you drove me nuts.''

''But aren't you glad I did?'' She laughed, a ripple of sound so purely carefree and happy that Mac knew a pang of envy.

''You're a lucky woman, Andrea.''

''Yes. I've found my true soul mate and that makes all the difference.''

''I'm glad for you.''

''I know.'' Turning her attention to the food on her plate, she changed the conversation to other things, and for the next hour they chatted with the comfortable ease of two people who'd waded through the misery of divorce, and managed to come out friends on the other side.

''Great breakfast, Andrea,'' he said, patting his midriff three waffles later. ''Tom had better watch his waistline, once you're married.'' He glanced at his watch and saw it was after ten already. ''I'd better get a move on. We're flying down to Los Angeles at two and I still have to pack and check out of the hotel.''

''I'll walk you down to your car.'' She took his arm and strolled with him from her apartment to the elevator. ''You know,'' she said, as they rode the twenty-two floors to street level, ''I was watching you dancing with Linda last night.

You had a look on your face that I've never seen before, as if you'd been given a gift beyond anything you'd ever expected. I'd hate to see you throw it away because you're too blind or pigheaded to recognize its worth.''

"Linda and I have known each other less than a week, Andrea!"

"But you've made love to her already, which—"

"How the hell do you know that?"

"You've made love to her already," she said calmly, unfazed by his outburst, "which tells me this is more than just your average casual affair. You don't allow yourself to get roped in that easily, Mac. You might recall that we dated for nearly three months before you slept with me."

"Only because your mother insisted on coming with us every time we went out!"

"Stop trying to turn this into a joke. You swore you'd never take on another investigation involving a missing child, yet here you are, up to your neck doing exactly that, simply because she asked you to. Why did you cave in so easily, I wonder?"

"Because succeeding where others have failed might ease my conscience, damn it, and make it possible for me to put the past to rest, once and for all!"

"How about because you couldn't say no to Linda?"

He stepped out of the elevator ahead of her without bothering to reply, because he didn't want to acknowledge the truth in her words.

That didn't silence her, though. Nothing could shut Andrea up if she felt like spouting off. "Don't punish yourself by chasing her out of your life because you think it's too soon to fall in love," she said, keeping pace with him as he strode through the foyer to the street. "It can happen in the blink of an eye. I think, in your case, it has. Why else are you so defensive about her?"

"I'm not the love-at-first-sight type."

"How do you know?"

He didn't, that was the whole trouble. Nor did he want to.

"At least, don't shut the door on the possibility. Allow yourself a little room for doubt."

"Oh, all right!" he said gruffly. "Anything for a quiet life!"

"I'm going to hold you to that, Detective." She stroked the hair back from his brow. "And either get a decent haircut, or find someone else to do this—like Linda, maybe. I've got a wedding to plan. Give her my best and take care of each other, okay?"

Scowling, he drove away. Andrea was annoying as hell, forever telling him how to run his life, and often too perceptive for her own—or his—good. But she was off base this time. The last thing he needed in his life was a bossy little witch like Linda Carr.

I'm your boss and you're fired....

Who the hell did she think she was, talking to him like that? The sooner this job wound up and he was rid of her, the better!

He called her room when he got back to the hotel, hoping she'd woken in a sweeter frame of mind than when she'd flounced off last night. But there was no answer, nor had she left him a message even though, before he went out for breakfast, he'd slipped a note under her door outlining their travel plans. Probably doing some last-minute shopping and hasn't noticed the time, he thought, throwing his things into his suitcase.

But when another hour had passed without any word from her, that old, familiar instinct kicked in again. *Something wasn't right.* He felt it in his bones.

Hauling along his baggage, he made a last trip to her door and found it propped open. He didn't need to look any further; the cart loaded with clean linens and supplies parked on the threshold told him she'd already vacated the room.

Even then, he hung on to the idea that she was somewhere in the hotel and paced the lobby looking for her. She was nowhere. Not curled up reading in one of the big comfortable chairs. Not browsing in the small arcade of shops near the rear entrance.

Finally he went again to the front desk, to inquire for the umpteenth time if she'd left word where she might be found.

The clerk, a different man from the one he'd spoken to before, seemed surprised he'd even ask.

"Ms. Carr checked out just after eight-thirty this morning, Mr. Sullivan," he said.

Mac stared at him, refusing to acknowledge what that might mean. "You must be mistaken."

"No, sir. I arranged for a taxi to take her to the airport. She caught the ten o'clock flight to Los Angeles." He reached into a pigeonhole on the wall behind him and handed Mac a folded slip of paper. "This message did just come in for you, though. Perhaps it will explain the mix-up."

But the note was not from her, it was from James Wagner. And what he revealed in a few succinct sentences made the waffles Mad had consumed for breakfast stir unpleasantly in the pit of his stomach.

His instinct regarding Sadie had been right on target. There was trouble brewing. And Linda was walking right into the thick of it.

He swung back to the desk clerk. "I need to charter a helicopter right away. Who do I call?"

She found the house just after one o'clock that afternoon. Three stories high, and tucked away at the end of a steep lane, it clung to the edge of a canyon, with a froth of bougainvillea spilling over its pale cream stucco walls.

Wicker furniture the same as that used by the Wagners in their San Francisco home lined wraparound balconies whose sliding glass doors stood open to let in the fresh ocean breeze. But it was the baby carriage on the lower porch that told Linda she'd finally run Kirk to earth.

Even as she watched from her post behind the palm tree next to the side gate, Linda saw a woman come from the house. Mexican, from the look of her, her skin a warm olive, the silver streaks in her dark hair shining in the brilliant sunshine. She peered into the carriage, rocked it gently and murmured softly, then turned to the man who appeared from around the corner.

Still breathless from the climb up the hill, Linda inched closer to the gate. Snatches of the conversation taking place less than thirty yards from where she stood drifted on the breeze. She didn't hear everything, but she heard enough. *Diapers* and *formula* might not prove conclusively that the baby in the carriage was Angela, but *Señor Thayer* left no doubt about the identity of the man dishing out orders to the nanny, who nodded obediently at his every word.

A thrill of excitement surged through Linda. She'd done it! She'd found her niece without Mac Sullivan's help, and if doing so didn't help to heal her bruised heart, it went a long way toward restoring her self-respect. She'd never needed a man to bail her out of a tight spot before, and her biggest mistake had been in thinking she needed one now.

Mac Sullivan had been an indulgence, and by the time he got here—always assuming he didn't become so involved with his ex-wife that he forgot he had a job to do— she'd be on her way back to Vancouver with her niece.

The only question was, exactly how to achieve that. Finding her way to the island and locating the Wagners' house had occupied most of her thoughts when she'd sneaked out of the Hyatt that morning, but now that she was actually here, and Angela was almost within touching distance, she didn't quite know what came next.

Marching up to the front door and demanding entry wasn't an option. She'd hardly be considered a welcome guest. The gate in front of her was locked, the walls on either side of it too high to scale. And even if she'd been able to climb over them, she couldn't see escaping the same way, with a baby in her arms.

Just then, Kirk Thayer swung away from the main house and cut across the tiled patio toward a small building set next to a second, wider gate at the foot of the garden. Shortly after, he emerged onto the road in a golf cart and chugged down the hill toward town.

No sooner had he disappeared than she darted around to the second gate and, to her joy and relief, found it unlocked. Perfect!

Before she lost her nerve, she slipped into the garden and hid in the lee of the outbuilding. Her heart was thundering, her palms clammy. The baby carriage stood not twenty paces away. It would take her no more than five seconds to race across the open space and seize the baby.

Unfortunately the nanny beat her to it, reappearing just as Linda was about to make a dash for it. Flattening herself against the building, she watched in horror as the woman scooped the baby into her arms and took her back into the house.

"Now what?" she whispered, wishing suddenly that she wasn't so alone. "What would Mac do, if he were here?"

Movement at a window on the top floor caught her eye. She saw the nanny cross to a nursery table clearly visible through the open slider. Watched as she changed Angela's diaper, then cradled her against her shoulder and stood a moment looking down the hill toward town, all the while crooning a lullaby in Spanish.

On the opposite side of the window, sunlight gleamed on the white rails of an infant crib. Linda waited, scarcely daring to breathe. Finally the nanny turned and lowered the baby to the mattress, adjusted the slats of the California shutters at the windows to diffuse the sun, and glided out of sight.

How long could she wait for the perfect opportunity, Linda wondered, vibrantly aware that Kirk could return at any minute and put paid to her plans. More to the point, wasn't the present setup about as perfect as she could expect, with the baby alone in her nursery and the nanny presumably occupied elsewhere?

She swept another quick glance over the garden, up at the house. Nothing stirred. Even the breeze had dropped to a whisper. "It's now or never," she breathed, and sprinted across the patio to the slider on the lower deck, directly below the nursery.

The room she entered likely belonged to the nanny. Spacious and pleasant, it held a bed, pretty dressing table, comfortable couch and a bookcase with a television set on top. Louvered doors on the wall to her right stood slightly ajar, revealing a walk-through closet with a bathroom beyond.

Opening another door on the opposite wall, Linda found herself in a long hall. Somewhere close by, a clothes dryer hummed. She heard footsteps on the tiled floor, and water running into a sink. Ordinary, tranquil noises, just loud enough to camouflage any sound she might make as she stole as far as the next room and squinted through the crack in the door.

The nanny stood at a table, humming to herself as she folded laundry. Behind her was an ironing board, with an iron plugged into a socket on the wall. A blue bowl turned slowly in a microwave oven set on a long counter. A steaming cup of coffee stood on a small table. The nanny was there for the duration.

Circumstances weren't going to get much more favorable than this, Linda realized, slipping past the door and racing stealthily up the stairs at the end of the hall. Another flight led her from the main level to the third floor and, at last, to the nursery.

Pushing open the door, she crossed to the crib. The baby lay on her back, gazing at the colorful mobile swinging above her head. Blue eyes, a drift of fine blond hair, rose petal skin, tiny perfect hands and feet...

Linda's heart contracted with painful joy. This was

ne's daughter, all right! The resemblance was amazing. disputable.

She knew a powerful urge just to pick her up and run, it knew, too, that there were other things she had to take re of first. She had no supplies and babies needed to be ept comfortable. There were diapers stacked on the lower elf of the change table, extra sleepers and receiving blankets in the drawers of the little white dresser, and a diaper ag hanging from a hook in the closet. Moving swiftly, she llected enough items to last until she could shop, and ssed them in the bag.

Then, slinging it over her shoulder, she approached the rib a second time. "Come here, precious," she cooed, ending over the baby. "I'm taking you home to mommy."

She was within a hairsbreadth of holding her niece in her rms when cool breath floated over the back of her neck.

"I don't think so, dear," a voice said softly in her ear. I think she prefers to stay with daddy."

Linda spun around and there he was, Kirk Thayer in the esh, big, rather bloated, and with a face the color of porrdge. *Good grief!* was her first thought. *What in the world ad June ever seen in the man?*

"Forget it, Mr. Thayer," she retorted, amazed that she ounded so calm when her insides were quaking with fright. I'm taking her back where she belongs and I'd like to see ou try to stop me."

"Would you, dear?" he said. "What will it take to convince you that I can? This, perhaps?"

He reached into his pocket and pulled out a small gun. water pistol, no less!

She laughed in his face. "Aren't you a bit too old to be laying with toys?

He blinked slowly and a thread of fear wound down her ine. He had the eyes of a madman. Pale gray like the cales of a fish too long dead.

He raised the pistol, aimed it at the open window and red. The noise it made, though not overly loud, was un-

mistakably deadly. "Do not irk me, dear," he said. "I ten
to overreact when I am irked."

I should have waited for Mac, she thought, her min
whirling with sudden terror. *He'd never have let this hap
pen. We'd be on our way back to the mainland by now, an
Angela would be safe.*

"I was expecting two of you," Kirk went on, conve
sationally. "What happened to your husband? Did he los
his nerve at the last minute?"

"How did you know to expect us at all?"

"My dear mother phoned and told me. She seemed t
think you might wish me ill. Just as well I picked up m
messages this morning, or you might have been gone befor
I realized what you were about."

Mac's voice echoed through her mind, his words as clea
as if he stood next to her in the room. *Sadie's a loos
cannon, Linda. ...a mother who's been overprotective a
her life....*

Why hadn't she believed him?

"I confess I didn't know you'd married," Kirk said, idl
stroking the barrel of the gun, "but I recognized your nam
at once. I heard it *ad nauseam* when June and I were sti
together. *Linda this, Linda that,* all day long. She's the on
who sent you here, of course, but it won't do her, or yo
any good. No one's taking Angela away from me."

"That's not why I'm here," she said, though such a lin
of reasoning was hardly likely to convince him. "June ju
wants to be sure Angela's thriving. She's not interested i
cutting you out of your daughter's life."

"Of course she is!" He shook his head sadly. "I'm s
disappointed in her. I really thought she understood. Afte
all, she grew up without a father, so she knows what a chil
misses, not having him there to guide her. It's what dre
us together in the first place, you know—the fact that we'
both been abandoned by a parent."

"And it can be the bond that keeps you together, Kirk.

"Don't make me laugh! She's sent you to steal m

daughter, but I'm not about to lose another child.'' He waved the gun, menacingly. ''You will not take her!''

''How are you going to stop me?'' she asked, swallowing the bile rising in her throat.

''Kill you, I suppose.''

He spoke as casually as someone else might have commented on the weather, and that, by itself, made Linda's blood run cold.

But, *Mentally unstable,* Sadie had said.

Off his rocker, James had declared.

How true!

She'd never thought that finding the baby would be easy. She'd been prepared for delays and setbacks. And the possibility of failure had always lurked in the back of her mind, waiting to make a sneak attack during a weak moment. But never for a second had she suspected the search might end in death.

It was obscene, she thought, her gaze swinging from Kirk to the rest of the room. Everything was too pretty. Too rich. Too *civilized!* Men bent on murder lurked in back alleys. They operated under cover of night. They did not flaunt their evil in bright sunshine, with people passing by on the street not thirty yards away.

''Are you going to shoot me?'' she asked, some small sliver of her brain remembering that, in the movies, the secret always was to buy time by keeping the villain talking.

''Heavens no, dear! You'd make a dreadful mess on the rug,'' he said cheerfully. ''You're going to fall over the balcony railing. Not right outside the nursery, of course. There's a much better spot around the side of the house, facing onto the canyon. It could be weeks before your body's discovered, if ever.''

''You'll never get away with it. Mac will come looking for me. He knows I'm here.''

''He can look all he likes, he won't find you. And he won't find me or my daughter, either. We'll be gone before your poor broken body stops rolling down the cliff. Rosa is already preparing for our little vacation. So come along, dear. Say goodbye to my little daughter and let's get this show on the road. No point in putting off the inevitable.''

She couldn't go near the crib again. Dare not, not with a madman waving a gun in her face. She made do with blowing a kiss across the room, then turned away.

He stalked her across the floor to the slider. ''That's a good girl,'' he said, nudging the pistol in her ribs to keep her moving. ''Turn to the right now, and keep on going. I'll tell you when to stop.''

The balcony curved, swinging away from the garden and veering toward the east where the steep sides of the canyon cut into the hillside. ''All right, dear, that's far enough,'' he decreed, prodding her forward from behind. ''Just climb onto the railing, and I'll give you a little push. Before you know, it will all be over.''

Searching for a possible means of escape, she stepped closer and glanced down—a huge mistake on her part. The world below dropped away too suddenly, leaving her blind with panic and clawing at the air for support. Even with her feet still firmly planted on solid ground, supernatural forces threatened to raise her up and fling her into the endless blue space of sky and sea. Already her lungs were bursting from the impact.

''Move, Linda!'' Kirk Thayer snarled, ramming the pistol against her spine.

''No,'' she panted. ''You're going to have to pick me up and bodily throw me over.''

She felt the muzzle of the pistol at the side of her throat; heard a deadly click. The safety catch being released? She didn't know. She'd never been this close to a gun before; couldn't tell the difference between the real thing and a toy.

I should have listened to you, Mac, she thought hopelessly. *I should have trusted you.*

But she had not. She'd sulked like a child and run off by herself to teach him a lesson. And now she was paying the price. But the worst of it was, so would he. Because of her rash actions, he would have another tragedy on his conscience; another blot on his personal record of achievement.

I'm so sorry, she told him, closing her eyes the better to bring his face into focus, and remembering how safe she'd felt when he held her in his arms. She hadn't known the meaning of fear then. It had not existed for her. He had not allowed it.

He was already inside the house when the gunshot shattered the serenity of the afternoon, and his heart literally stopped. But then, from the kitchen on the main floor, he heard the sound of voices—Thayer's and Linda's—and realized they came from the infant monitor on the counter.

Grabbing the laundry basket she carried, he shoved his way past the terrified woman staring at him from midway down the stairs, and raced to the top floor, guided by the sound of the baby's crying. Beyond the sliding glass doors, a cantilevered deck followed the curve of the house. The second he stepped outside, he heard Linda again.

"Why don't you just shoot me and get it over with, Kirk?" she said, her voice drifting, thin with terror, from somewhere to the right. "It's the only way you're going to be rid of me."

Don't give him ideas, cookie! Mac telegraphed, flattening himself against the wall and rounding the corner silently. *He's crazy enough already.*

He saw them at once. Saw Thayer climbing on top of the wide railing and dragging her up behind. He saw the pistol, too. Recognized its lethal capabilities.

He'd been a cop. He'd lost colleagues, faced death. Inflicted it even, when he had to. Never, though, in all those years, had he experienced anything to equate with the barren fear curdling his blood at that moment; a fear so profound that he recoiled from the shock of it.

Letting fly with a great roar of rage, he lunged forward and hurled the laundry basket. For an endless second, it seemed to hang in midair, its trajectory caught in a dream-like arc. Baby things fluttered lazily through the air. A little blanket bordered in pink satin glided like a parachute and draped itself over Thayer's hair.

He half turned, took the weight of the basket on the shoulder, staggered a moment, then tumbled almost gracefully into space, still clutching his pistol. But Linda, thank God, fell the other way, landing with a soft thump on the balcony, and crawling forward on her hands and knees until Mac could scoop her up into the safety of his arms.

It was late afternoon before the police finished questioning them.

"We can leave now," Mac told Linda, coming on her in the nursery where she sat in a rocking chair with the baby in her arms. "Pack up enough stuff to see her through the next few hours, and let's get out of here."

He might as well have been speaking in foreign tongues for all the notice she took, and he knew from her blank stare that the full effects of shock had finally hit.

"Hey, cookie," he said gently, dropping to one knee beside her and stroking her face. "It's over. Angela's safe. Thayer won't be bothering June, or you, or anyone else, ever again. You can go home now."

"I've never heard a person die before. I thought he'd never stop screaming."

"I know," he said, wanting to take her in his arms again so badly he could taste it. "It takes some getting used to, even for a hard-bitten guy like me."

"It's my fault he's dead." A flicker of some dark emotion passed over her face. "He wanted *me* to jump over the railing, but I couldn't."

"I know, darlin', and I'm glad you couldn't."

"Just looking down made me dizzy."

"I know," he said again. "You don't like heights."

She shuddered and brought the baby to snuggle against her neck. "Poor little baby! He startled her so badly when he fired his gun. She almost jumped out of her skin."

"He scared the living daylights out of me, as well. I was afraid he'd shot you."

"No," she said. "He was just showing me how it worked. I thought it was a toy, you see."

Some toy! "It was a nine millimeter Beretta, Linda. Pistols don't come much deadlier than that. He meant business."

Her eyes clouded with sorrow. "Poor Sadie!"

Poor Sadie nothing! "She's the one who blew the whistle on us."

"I know." She bit her lip, trying not to cry. "Because she loved him. He was *her* baby. When she hears what's happened to him—"

"You can't worry about that," he told her. "She's got James to lean on, and you've got enough to deal with. Come on, now, cookie. Collect what you think the baby's going to need, and let's get moving. There's a helicopter on standby in town, waiting to ship us over to LAX. We don't want to miss that flight to Vancouver."

"Will I have to come back here for the inquest?"

"No." He cupped her elbow and urged her to her feet. "I'll look after all that and tie up any loose ends. It's part of what you hired me to do."

Moving as if she were in a trance, she strapped the baby in her infant seat, and collected diapers, a couple of terry-cloth sleepers, a soother—all the stuff that new mothers carry with them wherever they go—while he went looking for formula, which he found already made up in bottles, in the refrigerator.

Finally, as the sun went down in an orange blaze, they reached the waiting helicopter and were off. "Don't look," he said, as the island dropped away below them.

For the first time in what seemed like years, she smiled and turning toward him, fixed her lovely blue-green eyes on him instead. He couldn't look her in the face. Wasn't ready to confront the feelings she stirred in him. It would be a mistake to try to put them into words. He might end up saying things he'd regret later.

"Where's your luggage?" he asked instead.

"I stowed it in a locker at the airport."

"We'll collect it first, then pick up the tickets."

"How soon does our flight leave?"

"At eight. You'll sleep in your own bed tonight."

"Mom will be surprised to see us."

"No, she won't," he said. "I phoned and told her the good news. The whole gang will be waiting at the other end, including June and your dad. It'll be quite the home-coming."

The baby started fussing just then, and kept her occupied for the duration of the trip. It wasn't until they'd arrived at the airport and he handed her her tickets at the security gate that she said, "Where's yours, Mac? And how come you didn't check your bags with mine?"

"I'm not coming with you, cookie."

"Why not?"

"Things to do here," he said. "All those loose ends I mentioned."

"Is that the only reason?"

"The job's just about over, Linda."

"To hell with the job!" she said, with something like her usual fire. "What about you and me?"

He shook his head. "This isn't the time for any of that."

Her shoulders slumped and her eyes filled with tears. "Is there ever *going* to be a time for us?"

"I can't answer that. All I know is that we both need to step back from everything that's happened this last week. It's been a real roller-coaster ride, and we need to catch our breath. Return to normal, to the lives we thought we wanted before you landed on my beach and everything started going haywire."

"You don't care how I feel about you?" she asked, her voice barely above a whisper.

"You don't *know* how you feel about me, that's my

whole point. You're so emotionally exhausted, you don't know what day of the week it is.''

"I'm willing to find out.''

"I'm not," he said, feeling about as low as dirt, but knowing he had to spell things out exactly as they were. "You put your life on hold to recover Angela, and so did I. It's time now to pick up where we left off. You've got family issues to resolve, ambitions to fulfill. I've got deadlines looming. I'm not willing to compromise any of them for something as elusive as…whatever it was we had this past week, and you shouldn't be, either.

"I thought we had something special.''

He heard heartbreak in her words; felt an answering tug of pain deep inside himself. "We did. I'll never forget it, or you. But it would be a mistake to blow it up into something more than it really was.''

Another voice intruded, advising passengers traveling on Flight 549 to Vancouver that boarding had commenced. "That means you, cookie," he said, nudging her gently toward the gate.

At the last minute, she turned and lifted her face to his. "I hate goodbyes.''

"Me, too," he said, and dropped a kiss at the corner of her mouth. "But we always knew we were a team just for a short while.''

For a moment, she clung to him, and he heard her tattered breathing and knew how close she was to breaking down. He couldn't have dealt with that so, coward that he was, he pushed her again toward the gate and without waiting to see that she passed through safely, wheeled around and left.

CHAPTER TWELVE

LIFE went on, Linda discovered, but it was never quite the same again. For some, like her parents, things were better. After years of being apart, they'd regained what they'd lost for so long and found each other again.

For June, too, the future looked bright. Motherhood brought a bloom to her face, to her spirit, which nothing could erase. Angela was well named; truly an angel and an endless source of delight to her doting family. It didn't hurt any that the boy next door came home from overseas a man, and picked up where his high school relationship with June had left off when his company shipped him off to Malaysia for six years.

For Linda, the adjustment wasn't so easy. Although happy for her mother and sister—and yes, for her father, too—being exposed to so much conjugal bliss was painful. So, she moved into her own apartment, across town from the rest of her family, and worked with one of the best chefs in North America, in one of the city's foremost hotels.

She went out with Melissa, to the movies, to restaurants. She kept a chart of ideas she might one day use when she opened her own place. The trouble was, the prospect didn't excite her very much anymore.

For a while—for too long—she hoped the phone would ring and it would be Mac, telling her he couldn't live without her. But he didn't call. He didn't visit. He sent one of his brothers to deliver her car and drive the Jaguar back to Oregon. As November gales swept away the last remnants of autumn, he sent a letter reiterating everything he'd said at the airport.

Kirk Thayer's death was ruled accidental, he wrote.

Sadie had a bit of a breakdown when she heard he'd died, so James took her off on a six-month cruise to the Far East. It'll do them both a world of good.

Trillium Cove's hunkered down for the winter. I'm working on a new book. Hope you, too, are moving forward with your career and that you're happy again.

She tore the paper into shreds and flushed it down the toilet. Then she lowered the lid and sat there crying her eyes out for a good half hour. Her mistake, she realized, had been allowing herself to fall in love with the man, when he'd never been anything other than the detective, there to meet a challenge and emerge victorious.

He'd moved on with his life. It was time she did the same with hers.

In December, she met a man who lived in her new building and started dating him. His name was John and he worked for the government. A nice, stable, steady guy whose idea of excitement was playing Scrabble—until the night he had one too many rum eggnogs and tried to put the moves on her.

She smacked him in the mouth and didn't go out with him again.

Christmas came and went. And still she dreamed about a man with too-long black hair, and blue-gray eyes, and a smile that turned her molten with longing. She heard his voice in her sleep, felt his touch on her body. And woke up with tears rolling down her face.

She ached, and didn't know what to do to stop the pain.

Things weren't the same. He'd gone from being contentedly alone, to being miserably lonely. The house was too big, the bed too empty. He spent too many hours standing at the big window in the living room, staring down at the wind-swept beach as if he expected to find her perched on a rock, staring through the curtains of rain to the mist-shrouded horizon. On the few occasions that a knock came at his door, his heart lifted, only to thud back in place when the caller turned out not to be Linda.

Andrea told him he was a fool. His brothers thought it was hilarious that a woman had finally brought him to heel. His sisters-in-law baked him pies and cookies and casseroles. His mother was wise enough to do none of those things.

He flew to Mexico for Christmas, to Ciudad del Carmen, to do some scuba diving and soak up a little sun. He met a pretty, fun-loving woman, and took her to bed, hoping she'd make him forget. She didn't. He couldn't get it up.

In February, the couple who owned the Trillium Cove Inn retired, and put the place on the market. Just as well. It had been going downhill for some time and needed an injection of fresh blood. Someone young and energetic, with sophisticated tastes and a cosmopolitan approach. Someone like Linda.

The Inn needed her.

He needed her.

She'd just finished shampooing her hair, one Saturday morning in early March, when the phone rang. Probably Melissa wanting to meet for lunch and do some shopping, she thought, lifting the receiver.

"Hey, cookie!"

Her heart leaped. Stopped. Soared and dipped like a gull riding the wind which scoured the beach below his house. "Who is this?" she said, afraid to say his name; afraid this was just another dream. It couldn't be him. He'd said they should get on with their separate lives. He'd never call, not after all this time.

"Who do you think it is?" he said, all tough Detective Lieutenant spitting the words out like bullets. "Who else do you know who calls you 'cookie'?"

She held the phone away. Stared at it. Brought it back to her ear. "What do you want?"

"Well, I've been thinking," he said. "This business of

living by myself has its drawbacks and you once told me I should hire a live-in housekeeper to take care of the cooking and laundry and all that sort of stuff. Trouble is, I can't find anyone who'll agree to my terms.''

"Perhaps you haven't looked hard enough.''

"I've scoured the state,'' he assured her. "It's not the cooking or the laundry that's the problem, it's the live-in part, given that I have only one bedroom and one bed. So I'm wondering if you'd be interested in the job, since you've already tried out the bed and me, and found both to be—''

"No, Mac,'' she said, a very small part of her laughing because she knew what he was really asking, but a much larger part bleeding because, for all *his* courage under fire, he didn't have the guts to come out and say what he really meant—and what she needed to hear. "I'm afraid not.''

"Tell me you're kidding!''

"I'm afraid not. Your terms just aren't good enough.''

"Well, I'll be damned! Are you open to negotiation?''

"Possibly. But it'll take more than a phone call to convince me to give it serious consideration.''

"I see,'' he said.

The phone clicked in her ear and the line went dead. Stunned, she replaced it in its cradle, unable to believe he'd actually hung up on her; that he'd opened up all her half-healed wounds and left her bleeding. Again!

Someone rapped on her door. Still flabbergasted, she went to answer. *He'd hung up on her!* After all this time— all this…this *silence,* he called out of the blue and just expected she'd fall in with whatever he suggested!

He stood outside in the hall, phone in one hand, flowers in the other. "Damn, but you're a difficult cuss,'' he said, jamming his foot in the door as if he thought she might slam it closed in his face—which she would have, if she hadn't been too paralyzed with joy to move! "I knew from the start I'd have my hands full dealing with you.''

"You can't be here,'' she said faintly, afraid she was

going to pass out. Afraid he was just a figment of her over-wrought imagination. "You're in Oregon."

His eyes glimmered with laughter. "I'm a genius, I know, but even I can't be in two places at once, cookie."

She leaned forward. Dared to touch him. He felt real enough. "You *are* here!"

"Well, sure," he said, looping an arm around her waist. "You did say a phone call wasn't enough, didn't you?"

She opened her mouth. Left it open. Because, for all that she wanted to say something significant, there were no words to describe how she felt. Like a perfectly risen soufflé just out of the oven. So light of spirit, so full of sudden elation that she wasn't sure she could stand herself. "You're here!" she said again, just to be sure, then, as an afterthought, "How did you find out where I live?"

"I phoned your mother. And I had to come."

"Why?"

"To tell you that a world without you in it isn't a place I want to be."

"That's not what you said in Los Angeles."

He backed her into the apartment and kissed her, hard and long. "What'll it take to make you forget what I said in Los Angeles?" he murmured against her mouth.

"A very great deal," she informed him, willing herself not to cave in if, at the end of it all, he just walked away and left her to start the healing process all over again. "You said we had nothing in common, that our priorities didn't coincide."

"Is it okay for me to be wrong, once in a while?"

She regarded him warily. "I don't know. It depends."

"Would it reassure you if I told you I came here with more than just empty promises?" He dropped the flowers on the table and pulled her down beside him on the sofa. "I have a proposition for you, cookie."

"I'm listening," she said, absorbing the sight and scent of him. He wore tan slacks and a tan leather jacket, with a black turtleneck sweater underneath. He'd had his hair cut recently. He'd splashed aftershave on his freshly shaven jaw. She could have eaten him up.

"Tell me first, have you done anything about starting your own restaurant?"

"No," she said, steeling herself to resist the idea of abandoning all her ambitions and dreams just to be with him.

"Why not? Don't you want your own business after all?"

"Yes. I've worked too hard to give up on it. It's the only thing I know I can count on."

"You can count on me, Linda," he said. "And I won't ask you to give up a thing by doing so. I'll give you the world if you'll let me."

"I don't need the world, Mac," she said, drowning in the stormy blue-gray of his eyes. "I never did."

"How about a piece of my world, then? A house on the beach, with the Trillium Cove Inn thrown in on the side? I bought it, cookie, but I'm damned if I know what I'm going to do with it, if you won't agree to accept it as a wedding gift."

"I'm not getting married," she said on a fragile breath, even as her heart soared again.

"Would you, if I were to propose?"

"It would depend."

He drew her closer. Let his lips graze lightly, teasingly, over hers. "On what, darlin'?"

"On why you asked," she said, struggling to inhale a puff of air into her beleaguered lungs.

"Would telling you I love you be enough?"

"Do you?" she asked him.

"Oh, honey, you have no idea! And nor had I for the longest time. Yes, I love you." He leaned closer, lifted a strand of her wet hair and put his mouth to her ear. "The plain truth is, no one makes me fulminate like you."

She dared to laugh then, and it felt wonderful. All the grief and misery simply melted away in the sunshine of his answering smile as if they'd never been anything but a brief and passing storm. "Did you really buy the Inn?"

"Uh-uh. Like me, it's in pretty sad shape and desperate for some TLC." He kissed her earlobe, teased the outer shell of her ear with his tongue. "Probably requires a new kitchen, definitely needs a new chef."

"I think we can probably work out some sort of deal," she said, fighting a losing battle with the desire taking hold within her. How many times had she relived that night in San Francisco? How often had she imagined his touch again? Dreamed of surfing the waves of passion with him, and knowing that he needed her as badly as she needed him?

Too often! It was time to experience them in the flesh. "In fact," she said, "the more I think about it, running an inn by day, and fulminating with you by night seems like a very fine idea."

"I'm not an easy man, Linda," he reminded her soberly. "It won't always be smooth sailing. I get moody when the writing's not going well. Impossible to deal with when old colleagues call on me for advice, then ignore it. I have a past and people from it who still matter to me."

"Are you trying to talk me out of it already?"

"Not a chance." He inched her back against the sofa cushions, and traced the shape of her mouth with his finger. "No matter what else happens, I promise you'll always come first. You'll never face another day, or another difficulty, without me there beside you."

"I know that," she whispered, pulling him down until his weight rested against her and she could feel the erratic tattoo of his heart against hers. "And it's *all* I need to know. I love you, Mac Sullivan, because of who you are—because of your loyalty and your strength and your compassion. Please remind me of that if I ever forget it again."

"You can count on it, cookie," he said, his gaze scouring her face, feature by feature. "And at the risk of repeating

yself, I'll say it again: you can also count on me. Always
d forever.''

It was more than she'd dared to hope for. And all she'd
ver want.

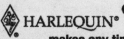

Season's Greetings

from

HARLEQUIN®
Presents~

Seduction and Passion Guaranteed!
The world's bestselling romance series.

Treat yourself to a gift this Christmas!
Enjoy these holiday stories,
written especially for you:

CHRISTMAS EVE WEDDING
by Penny Jordan #2289

CHRISTMAS AT HIS COMMAND
by Helen Brooks #2292

THE PLAYBOY'S MISTRESS
by Kim Lawrence #2294

All on sale in December

Pick up a Harlequin Presents® novel
and you will enter a world of
spine-tingling passion and provocative,
tantalizing romance!

Available wherever Harlequin books are sold.

HARLEQUIN®
Makes any time special®

International bestselling author

SANDRA MARTON

invites you to attend the

WEDDING *of the* YEAR

Glitz and glamour prevail in this volume
containing a trio of stories in which
three couples meet at a
high society wedding—and
soon find themselves
walking down the aisle!

Look for it in November 2002.

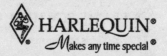

A visit to Cooper's Corner offers the chance for a new beginning...

Coming in December 2002
DANCING IN THE DARK
by Sandra Marton

Check-in: When Wendy Monroe left Cooper's Corner, she was an Olympic hopeful in skiing...and madly in love with Seth Castleman. But an accident on the slopes shattered her dreams, and rather than tell Seth the painful secret behind her injuries, Wendy leaves him.

Checkout: A renowned surgeon staying at Twin Oaks can mend Wendy's leg. But only facing Seth again—and the truth—can mend her broken heart.

The world's bestselling romance series.

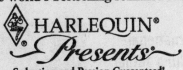

HARLEQUIN®
Presents

Seduction and Passion Guaranteed!

Introducing Jane Porter's exciting new series

**The Galván men: proud Argentine aristocrats...
who've chosen American rebels as their brides!**

IN DANTE'S DEBT
Harlequin Presents #2298

Count Dante Galván was ruthless—and though it broke Daisy's
heart she had no alternative but to hand over control of her family's
stud farm to him. She was in Dante's debt up to her ears! Daisy
knew she was far too ordinary ever to become the count's wife—
but could she resist his demands that she repay her dues in his bed?

On sale January 2003

LAZARO'S REVENGE
Harlequin Presents #2304

Lazaro Herrera has vowed revenge on Dante, his half brother, who
refuses to acknowledge his existence. When Dante's sister-in-law
Zoe arrives in Argentina, it seems the perfect opportunity. But
the clash of Zoe's blond and blue-eyed beauty with his own
smoldering dark looks creates a sexual force so strong that
Lazaro's plan begins to fall apart....

On sale February 2003

**Pick up a Harlequin Presents® novel and you will enter
a world of spine-tingling passion and
provocative, tantalizing romance!**

Available wherever Harlequin books are sold.

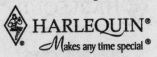

HARLEQUIN®
Makes any time special ®

Visit us at www.eHarlequin.com

HPGALVAN